MERCY,
PITY,
PEACE
AND
LOVE

MERCY, PITY, PEACE AND LOVE

Stories by

Rumer and Jon Godden

William Morrow and Company, Inc.
New York

c1989

Library of Congress Cataloging-in-Publication Data

Godden, Rumer, 1907–
  Mercy, pity, peace and love : stories / by Rumer and Jon Godden.
      p.   cm.
  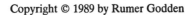ISBN 0-688-08630-6
  I. Godden, Jon, 1906–1984. II. Title.
PR6013.02M4   1990
823'.912—dc20   89-48720
                                                          CIP

Printed in the United States of America

First Edition

1   2   3   4   5   6   7   8   9   10

For Sarasvati

Contents

Foreword

'*Bhadra kalyai namonityam Sarasvatyai nama namaha. Bhadra kalyai namonityam Sarasvatyai nama namaha . . .* ' '*Worship and follow Sarasvati. Praise her name.*'

Sarasvati is India's goddess of pen and ink; even as children she was our favourite partly because, unlike other Hindu goddesses, Sarasvati is not always multiple-armed but usually modelled as a graceful young woman with flowing black hair; she is dressed in a tinselled sari and holds a *vina*, the beautiful stringed instrument like a long-necked guitar made from a gourd. Beside her is a swan, her symbol.

Sarasvati is not only the Goddess of pen and ink but of painting, sculpture, music, acting, dancing, all the arts, which is fitting as she is the consort of Brahma, god of creation and first person of the Hindu trinity: Brahma, the creator, Vishnu, the preserver, and Shiva, the destroyer, who is also the resurrection.

On Sarasvati's feast day, Vasanti Panchnami, an image of her is set up in a *pandal** in almost every bazaar or street throughout Bengal; students, artists, schoolchildren

---

* *Pandal*: a pavilion.

can bring their books, texts and paintings to lay them at her feet.

This is where I should like to put these stories because, though some of them are not Hindu but Moslem or Christian in feeling, they belong to her, various as they are.

Of course they are varied, India is not a country, as we are apt to think of it, but a continent and a contradictory continent. She holds every kind of countryside, every kind of climate from hot deserts to snows. There is every kind of flower, gentians and edelweiss as well as marigolds, frangipani and hibiscus, every kind of people from the darkest of Aboriginals to the fair-skinned Kashmiris; from illiterates to Parsees who are perhaps the most cultured and sophisticated people in the world. There are four chief religions of India and many cults in each; thirteen major languages – more than forty if the dialects are counted – so that a man in the south speaking Telegu cannot understand his fellow in the north speaking Urdu or Punjabi.

Though several of these stories were written years ago they are not, as many people might assume since we are English and were born in the days of the British Empire, stories of the Raj – neither as children nor as young women had we heard that term. They are, simply, of India, some, like Jon's 'The Carpet', of an India that is changing – Kashmir is now a tourist Mecca though still, far from the accustomed routes, there are weddings, as in 'Red Doe', still nomad tribes, *bakriwars* or 'goat people' on the march, as in 'The Little Black Ram', while Jon's Calcutta stories and my 'Mercy, Pity, Peace and Love' could be, and probably are, happening today.

Forty years ago when I went to India for the making

of the film of my book *The River* with Jean Renoir, greatest of all film directors, his largely Indian crew insisted that filming should begin on Vasanti Panchnami. 'Most auspicious,' they said.

A special *pandal* was put up in the main room of the house at Barrackpore, just outside Calcutta, that we were using as a studio; supported on cut banana trees with their wide green leaves, the *pandal* was draped with red muslin and hung with garlands of flowers and mango leaves. The cameras were blessed as the crew, with drums and tiny percussion cymbals, chanted and, on behalf of the Company, but more especially as a writer, I had to lay the book and my script at her feet.

Now, far away from India, in the quiet of my small study, for myself and for Jon, in spirit I do that again; 'Please, Sarasvati, bless this book.'

'Bhadra kalyai namonityam Sarasvatyai nama namaha. Bhadra kalyai namonityam Sarasvatyai nama namaha.'

Rumer Godden
Moniaive
Dumfriesshire
Scotland

BENGAL

Bengal River

Poem

Nothing can mollify the sky,
the river knows
only its weight and solitude, and heat, sun-tempered cold,
and emptiness and birds: a boat: trees, fine white sand,
and deltas of cool mud: porpoises: crocodiles:
and rafts of floating hyacinth, pools and water-whirls
and, nurtured in blue mussel shells, the sunset river pearls.

The boat hovers over the mussel beds,
and for these the divers go
naked into the water to work with nets and naked hands.
Split open the shell, the pearl is another world
evolved, revolved from a grit, and here, where the sky is vast,
the ball of the planet turns, flat below space, finite,
and is lost in the infinite worlds of the infinite stars of the night.

Here in the river is life,
life in the diver and pearl,
life in the wings of the bird, in the boat that is painted with eyes,
in the porpoises, joyously turning, wet and blue in the sun,
and the river is Ganges water with a ritual life of its own;
along its curious serrated banks in the grasses grow pygmy trees
flowered by the pollen balls that honey the hot breeze.

This, its indigenous life,
but there it ends;
there is no generosity in the sky, in the abstract tiger land.
The finality of the pearl, the gentleness of the flowers,
are evenly swept away; the boat of itself floats down,
till the nets are lifted and gone and the fangs of the night
    come again
and the little influence of daylight is lost along the plain.

Possession

The ricefield lay furthest from the village, nearest to the road. On all sides the plain unrolled in the sun under a pattern of white clouds, white pampas grass in autumn, white paddy birds, and glimpses of sky-reflecting water from the *jheels* or shallow pools. The sky met the horizon evenly all the way round the flatness of the plain, an immense weight of sky above the little field but the old peasant, Dhandu, did not look at the sky, he looked at his field. He did not know that it was little; to him it was the whole world. He would take his small son, Narayan, by the wrist and walk with him saying, 'The field belonged to my grandfather and your great-grandfather; to my father and your grandfather; it is mine, it will be yours.'

'I shall be a ferryman when I grow up,' said little Narayan to his mother, Phalani. 'I shall be a postman, and bring you a letter every day.' After he went to the fair at Pasanaghar he wanted to be a sweet-seller. He would cry, '*Jelepis, sandesh*',* and show his tray. His tray was a leaf fallen down from the palm trees and the *jelepis* were rolled of clay and water, but his father took it seriously and said, 'No, son, you will be a cultivator like me and we shall work the field.'

---

* *Jelepis, sandesh*: Indian sweetmeats.

Narayan would nod his head with the sweat from playing still wet on his forehead and neck; then he wavered. 'I should like so much to drive a bus, Father.'

'You will be a cultivator.'

The pampas grass waved its plumes in autumn; in spring the hyacinth weeds in the water opened spiked flowers of fresh mauve, and the honey-scented balls of the thorn tree sent their sweetness down the path that led from the village through the ricefields to the road. After the rains the path baked slowly to a hard clay whiteness, smoothed by the passing and repassing of naked feet; it was on its smoothness that Narayan had learned to run with nothing to trip him and make him fall. In those days Phalani made a short coat of red cloth and tied strings with bells round his ankles, touched his eyes with kohl and oiled his sturdy back and thighs; he had been more beautiful and well grown than any little boy in the village. The anklet bells had tinkled as he ran, and the workers among the rice shoots raised their heads to look; Phalani's heart had swelled with pride and she smiled. Phalani's smile was like a water spring; it seemed to well up and flood her face, lips and eyes; she could only smile when she was proud and glad; she had no false smiles.

That was a long time ago in the village, but to Phalani it was now; if it was spring and the honey-scented balls bloomed, it was the same spring; the pampas grass waved, it was the same autumn; each year brought the same winter, the same heat and the same rains. Coming from the hut, carrying a bowl of curd or a *pān* leaf to Dhandu on his day-bed, she would look down the empty path. 'I want to be a ferryman when I grow up' . . . 'I will bring you a letter every day.'

'You will be a cultivator. Your grandfather . . . your

father . . . ' but Narayan had been a soldier and gone to the war.

'War. What is this war?' No one in the village knew what the war was, though the schoolmaster and the post-office clerk from Pasanaghar read the newspapers. To the villagers, Narayan and the young men from the villages round who had been recruited were, simply, gone. 'When will they come back?' the women asked. 'When will they come back?' The schoolmaster and the post-office clerk shrugged their shoulders.

'But what *is* war?'

'War is like locusts,' said the post-office clerk sententiously. 'Like a plague of locusts devouring . . . '

'But – locusts leave nothing . . . '

The schoolmaster and the post-office clerk shrugged their shoulders again.

Phalani felt they should know more of the war than that; as the mother of a soldier, she knew war was not locusts. She was timid but she spoke. 'In war,' she said, 'they have guns. My son has a gun.'

Guns. The only gun in the village was the great old blunderbuss with its single barrel as long as a *lathi** that they let off to scare the birds in the mango grove when the fruit was ripe. It did not scare the birds but once it had killed a dog.

The mango grove belonged now to Bijay Rai. Little by little, Bijay Rai had bought all the land in the village; now he was a big landowner; the only bit left in the village that was not his was Dhandu's field.

It was a beautiful field. Lying next to the road, it benefited from the slight incline that had come from

* *Lathi*: a wooden staff used by policemen.

11

the digging for water channels; the silt from the other fields washed down into it, and the silt was rich and the crop on Dhandu's field was always the best. Bijay Rai, Dhandu knew, would have given a great deal to buy the field and complete his ownership, but Dhandu's field was not for sale.

When it was warm in spring and in the hot summer evenings, Dhandu went down and sat beside his field, though the land was beautiful to him in any season. After the first planting out of the young shoots when all the fields showed a tender green; when the rice was grown and ready and the breeze made wind patterns paler and darker as the blades bent and the paddy birds waded like small cranes in the water; or at the beginning of winter when the rains had dried and the earth was ploughed and the weeds were heaped in small stacks in each field and set alight at dusk. Then, in the growing dark, the chequered lines of the small fields were lost, the oxen were driven home and, one after the other, the fires burned red and a spiral of white smoke went up from each. It was all life to Dhandu, and the health and strength of his land made health and strength in his veins and bones. He gazed at his crop and he felt safe; he had his land and he had a son; only one son, it was true, but Narayan had grown to a fine young man; with his army training he had grown broad and strong, his muscles swelled to hardness. His army pay was large; when Dhandu thought of Narayan's English cigarettes, the excellent leather of his belt and boots, the good wool of his khaki greatcoat, he was weak with wonder. Dhandu had never had a pair of shoes, only his village-made clogs with a peg between the toes; all they had in the house against the cold were quilts so old that the wadding had come through the thin cotton cloth, and a shawl, a *chuddhar*, that was cotton too; Dhandu's old bones did not know what it was not to be chilled just as his stomach did not know what it was to be filled. When Narayan laughingly put his army greatcoat on his father it seemed to Dhandu over-warm and heavy. Narayan said he would send Dhandu an army vest; he did not send the vest but the very thought of Narayan in the greatcoat made Dhandu warm; the thought of his son was a warm rich safe tide of life.

When Phalani felt the greatcoat with her finger and thumb she smiled; no more than Dhandu could she understand how her son came to wear it, and she knew she could not understand. The first time Narayan had come back from school he had shown her the slate on which the schoolmaster had written characters for him to learn; Phalani had looked at the marks on the slate as if her soul would rake out their meaning but, as fast as Narayan told her, she forgot. She could not remember I for *indur* from I for *igal*, not as much as A for *am* or U for *ut*. Ma, it's *easy*! Even little Monmatha knows it!' Phalani could not, and she did not care. She had always gone to meet Narayan after school; she still felt the warmth of his little wrist as she had led him nome. In all his growth she had felt his smallness, the babyhood that lies curled at the root of every man; Dhandu had felt the manhood in the baby.

'Wait,' said Dhandu. 'One day he will come and work with me in the field.'

When the telegram came that day the peon had wanted money. Dhandu had some pice in his waist knot. 'Give him one. Give him,' Phalani had begged. She had had a foolish idea that if the peon were given money he might take the telegram away. 'Give him a pice,' she begged but Dhandu was surly. 'I have nothing for him.'

'A *pice*! I want a rupee. It's a long ride to your dirty village,' called the peon but Dhandu would not give him anything and he had ridden away, his red bicycle wobbling on the path as he looked back to shout abuse. 'Will a jackal's cry kill a buffalo?' said Dhandu. The telegram, though, had been left. They had not known what to do with it until the schoolmaster and the clerk came running.

'Bad news,' said the schoolmaster and had snatched it. The clerk snatched it from the schoolmaster and tore it open; the schoolmaster snatched it from the clerk and finally it had come in two. By that time there was a crowd, some of them on the schoolmaster's side and some against him; it was not until later, in the hubbub, that the schoolmaster had turned to Dhandu and said, 'I am sorry, very sorry, to have to inform you that Narayan your son is dead.'

Dhandu had looked at them making this noise in his courtyard. Suddenly he had taken up a stick and driven them all out. '*Jao!* Get out of here! All of you and both of *you*,' he said to the schoolmaster and the clerk. 'Get out and never come back. Get out! Sons of pigs! *Jao!*'

It was soon after that, or perhaps not soon, next summer or next spring, that Bijay Rai had come to see Dhandu.

At first, to the village, it had seemed that Phalani was the most changed. It was true that Dhandu seemed to have grown old in the night; that he had no more strength in his legs and could only totter from the hut to his day-bed in the courtyard, but his face, his voice, his look were the same, while there began to be whispers about Phalani. She did her work in the hut and the courtyard and field, she tended Dhandu, but it was a husk of Phalani, a body without light, without a smile; it was not Phalani because Phalani was not there. 'She will go mad,' said the whispers. 'She is mad.' Then one day, Sukhdevi, the village midwife, had come into the hut and, without a word, put down in the corner a tiny spring bed with a rag for a quilt and a homemade mosquito curtain bordered with tinsel. Round the bed Sukhdevi arranged dolls' cooking-pots, and platters made of clay, and in the bed she put a little clay doll washed with white. 'Krishan ji Maharaj has come into your house,' she said. 'Mind you look after Him well.'

'Krishan!' whispered Phalani. '*Ma, I want to be a ferryman when I grow up . . .* ' '*It's easy! Even little Monmatha . . .* ' '*Ma . . . I shall bring you a letter every day.*' The anklet bells tinkled on the path. 'Narayan Rajah. Krishan.' Phalani put out her finger and touched the image of the little god.

Bijay Rai came to see Dhandu. Dhandu, helpless on the day-bed, greeted him with fierce pride. 'It grieves me to see your field,' said the crocodile, Bijay Rai. 'It grieves me.'

Dhandu did not answer. He stared at a crack in the courtyard earth through which a procession of black ants was crawling. From inside the hut he could hear Phalani singing, a soft nasal lullaby chant, and it seemed to him insane. Every moment of her day was passed now in a ritual of worship, tending the doll; for Him she kept the courtyard swept and washed, the hut so clean that the earth floor shone; there was fresh water in the pitchers, and the brass cups and platters were scrubbed to gold. For Him she decorated the steps and lintels with fresh patterns of white flour paste, and brought in marigolds; for Him she gathered dung and spread it on the wall in pats to dry for fuel, for Him she ground millet and cooked; she cooked rice and chapattis and a handful of vegetables until there was no more rice, no vegetables. Soon she and Dhandu were living on thinner and thinner chapattis and water seasoned with pepper. Phalani's strength was failing; though her devotion shone in her eyes her body was wasting; she could no longer work in the fields, and the hoe and the basket stood idle against the wall.

'I grieve to see your field,' said Bijay Rai.

Dhandu gazed at the ants as they filtered through the crack; in Dhandu himself a crack was widening and spreading. 'Why not let my men work the field?' said Bijay softly. 'That is better than letting it waste. We can share the crop, or, if you like, I shall pay you rent. You have nothing to live on,' said Bijay still more softly. 'A little money would be acceptable, yes?'

Dhandu looked proudly at the ants but the crack was growing wider; his hunger gnawed inside him and from inside the hut came that weak singing.

'Why should anything be difficult?' murmured Bijay Rai. 'We could arrange it as between friends . . . '

Dhandu raised his head. 'Bijay Rai, Sahib,' he said, 'I am not your friend.' Afterwards he was glad that he said that.

'*Ache bhai*,'* said Bijay Rai affably and went away. He soon came back. By that time Dhandu and Phalani were a great deal more hungry. Dhandu was so weak that he could hardly sit up. 'I have thought of something better,' said Bijay Rai. He sat down by Dhandu. 'I am your old friend and you do not trust me. I am deeply grieved.' He sat looking down at his black patent city shoes with the black patent-leather bows and sighed. 'I am deeply grieved,' and he looked at Dhandu out of his small eyes.

* *Ache bhai·* 'All right, brother' or 'Agreed, brother.'

'I am so grieved that I have thought of something,' said Bijay Rai. 'To prove myself to you I have decided to lend you two hundred rupees.'

'Two . . hundred · . ?' said Dhandu faintly.

'With it, as you do not trust me,' said Bijay Rai with bitterness but his little eyes twinkled, 'you may get labour and work your field. Do not thank me,' said Bijay Rai severely as Dhandu opened his mouth. 'I do not wish to be thanked. You can repay me when you sell your crop, and I shall take surety from you.'

'I have no surety to give,' said Dhandu.

'Do not give your hut,' said Bijay Rai. 'That would be foolish. In case of want you must always keep your home; you can do it on the field. It is nothing,' said Bijay Rai waving his plump hand and small gold ring. 'You will redeem it, of course, when the crop comes; then you will pay me off. The interest for that time is small and the money will last a long time. You will not notice it,' said Bijay Rai. 'A pure formality.'

'No,' said Dhandu but he knew with hunger he was weakening.

'In a year you will have paid me off,' said Bijay Rai, laughing gently. 'You will not need more than a tenth part for labour and a little for your subsistence. You need not spend the rest . . . ' but, without intention of spending, Dhandu spent the rest.

When he had put his mark on the paper Dhandu was so hungry, he no longer felt that twinge; Bijay Rai had not advanced as much as an anna until the paper was signed; it was a fair paper with a fair interest but, as soon as Dhandu was comfortably filled, more comfortably than for years, he knew that he had betrayed the field. He put away the thought. 'I shall get it back, *immediately*,' said

Dhandu. 'I shall go to Bijay Rai and say . . . ' He swelled as he thought of what he would say and how he would keep enough money to pay Sharma, his neighbour's son, to work the field for the second crop and a little back from that . . .

Once again the field was watered and planted and Dhandu was able, slowly, with his stick, to walk down the path and sit and watch the wind blow, dark and pale in the grown crop. He could see the crop was good. 'And I have most of the money left,' said Dhandu, 'there in the hole in the wall by the bed.'

There was so much money that he decided to repair the hut thatch and limewash the walls; Bijay Rai encouraged him. 'And I should clean out the well. The crop will be good and you can afford it. How many', he asked, 'have their own well? You should look after it. And mend the fence – or better, have a new fence. Sharma will do it for you with little expense. You can afford it. Why not do this?' asked Bijay Rai of one thing. 'Why not do that?' of another. His eyes shone. It was he who suggested the warm shawls. 'You are a land-owner,' said Bijay Rai; 'now you are old you should keep dignity.'

'My father never had a warm shawl,' said Dhandu. 'He had a *chuddhar*.'

'Your father never had two hundred rupees.'

'That is true,' said Dhandu. He bought a hen and a paraffin lamp; then he had to get a coop for the hen and buy oil for the lamp. Sharma needed a new basket. When the crop was harvested, and Dhandu and Phalani had taken what they needed, there was only a little left to be sold, and Sharma had to be paid; the second crop was poor and they ate it all. When the year was up Bijay Rai came.

'Well?' he asked.

'I cannot pay you.'

'Then at least pay me my interest.'

'Interest?' Dhandu lifted his head.

'Twenty rupees,' said Bijay Rai. 'You are lucky, the money-lender takes a hundred for every fifty.' And he shook and chuckled as if that amused him.

When the twenty rupees were taken out of the hole in the wall there was only a rupee and some small coins left. A year ago the two hundred rupees had seemed very large; now the twenty rupees seemed larger. 'It is a lot of money,' said Dhandu. He was reluctant to give it.

'It has been earned,' said Bijay. His voice snapped like a crocodile's jaws – or was that Dhandu's imagination?

'You said you would pay me rent and now I pay you rent – for my own field,' said Dhandu; he did not understand how that had come about.

At the end of the second year things were worse. There was nothing with which to pay Sharma, and the field lay uncultivated; shawls, lamp, hen, all were gone and it was strange how the value changed from when something was bought to when it was sold. The old hunger came back, and worse, for Dhandu was trying to scrape this year's twenty rupees; he scraped and saved, but however empty their stomachs, the hole in the wall remained empty as well.

'And if I can't pay you?' asked Dhandu.

'You will owe me two hundred and twenty rupees,' said Bijay Rai suavely. 'Next year you will owe me two hundred and forty-two, the year after two hundred and sixty-six, in eight years it will have doubled, which is more than the price of your field.'

Dhandu sat in his bed in the sun; he sat when Bijay Rai came, he preferred then to be upright but the rest of the time, nowadays, Dhandu lay down. The sun reached him but did not warm him; a terrible chill was in his bones. Dhandu began to shake. Bijay Rai shrugged his shoulders and left.

Presently Phalani came through the courtyard from the path; she walked slowly, with great weakness, but she was smiling. She had been to bathe herself, and her hair, freshly washed, was coiled neatly; she had washed her old sari too and dried it in the wind, and she carried oleander flowers. She walked with a lilting step, and the sun fell on her shoulders and made her shadow clear as she walked. Dhandu raised his head. 'Where are you going?'

'Inside.' She showed him the flowers and smiled, looking towards the hut. 'Then I must go to the bazaar,' she said and broke off and smiled again. 'There is a Nepali there, a trader. He has some little brass pots, real brass.' She showed him the size with her fingers. 'They are for children, but Krishan . . . Narayan . . . '

Dhandu's temper broke. Blindly he felt for his stick and tottered off the day-bed; he seized her by the shoulder and with angry strength he dragged her to the hut and up the patterned steps. 'You are a fool! Fool!' he shouted. 'Imbecile! Owl! Daughter of an owl! Narayan is dead. Dead!'

Inside the hut, in the gloom after the sun outside, he could see the saucer lamp, its wick burning in its earthenware bowl like a red spark before the little bed; no matter what they went without, Phalani found or begged the oil for this. The light shone on tinsel, flowers, cut-up fruit, grains of food. 'Fool! Fool!' cried Dhandu. 'Krishan! There is no Krishan. Narayan is dead. He is dead. We have lost the field. Narayan is dead,' and he lifted his stick and brought it down on the lamp, smashing its clay. The lighted oil ran out in a puddle of fire on the floor; Dhandu jerked the bed into it with his stick and the fire ran up the curtains, which curled up and burned green as the flame caught the tinsel; the little doll fell on his face, the food was scattered, and the clay pots broke. Dhandu stood leaning on his stick, gasping. 'Now do you understand?' said Dhandu. 'They have killed my son. They have taken away my land.'

Phalani did not answer; her fingers twitched, twitched, and her eyes never left his face.

There was the sound of voices and, from the path, two people came in and stood in the courtyard: a man in uniform and an Englishwoman. Dhandu hobbled to the doorway and looked glaringly down at them. Behind him Phalani went down on her knees and gathered up the broken pots.

'What do you want?' said Dhandu.

'We are the Indian Forces Families visitors,' began the man. 'Your son, Narayan . . . '

'I have no son, Narayan.'

The man looked at a card. 'Narayan Chand. WBX 13758.'

From behind Dhandu in the hut Phalani began to sing, the same lullaby, but broken, sobbing.

'What is that?' asked the woman, and they pushed past Dhandu to see.

Phalani had put the doll back in the bed and was straightening the burned curtains. She did not know the visitors were there. 'What is this?' the Englishwoman asked after a while.

'I think it must be the worship of Gopal, the Lord Krishna, in the shape of a child,' said the man in uncertain English. 'Very often it is made by childless women or those who have lost a child. They tend Him, look after Him. It has saved reason . . . '

'*Ma, it's easy. Even Monmatha knows that . . . Krishan, Krishan ji Maharajah. Narayan . . . Krishan . . .*' Phalani began to smile.

'She is quite happy,' said the man. 'She knows nothing at all.' And, turning to Dhandu, he began to explain about the pension.

'. . . Accumulated pension and there is gratuity owing, in all more than two hundred rupees, and you will receive a further monthly sum. You see, your son still looks after you,' said the man. 'In this way he has not died. But you should have had it more than two years ago. You should have *applied*,' said the man severely, and he said to the woman in English again, 'These people are helpless. Helpless! What fate sends them, they accept.'

When it was warm, in the spring, Dhandu hobbled down to sit beside his field. He saw it with its tender green, he would see it with the rice high, chased with its wind patterns; it would be harvested in the autumn, it would be ploughed, and weed fires would smoke in the evening. Dhandu did not look up at the sky or away to the great rim of the horizon; he looked at his field. Phalani, coming to fetch him, felt a small, warm wrist in her hand. 'Krishan. New little pots, real brass.'

She helped Dhandu to his feet and they stood side by side. They did not look at one another. Dhandu saw the field. Phalani saw her son. 'It won't be a good crop. The rains were too early,' Dhandu grumbled, but he smiled. He had his field.

'*Ma . . . I want to be a ferryman . . .*' Krishan. She had her son.

CALCUTTA

Rahmin

Rahmin was sent, or passed on to me by a friend. I opened her note on the verandah of my house and read: 'I don't suppose that you want another *chiken-wallah*,* but please buy something from Rahmin Mahomed if you can.'

In Calcutta, where I lived, the *chiken-wallahs* worked in rows of booths in the market or out in the nearby villages, whole families stitching away, fulfilling orders – if they were lucky – for monograms, children's dresses, table-linen, underclothes or, more often, making and embroidering these things. They would then be packed in a thin cotton cloth, made into a neat bundle, and carried to the houses of Europeans or wealthy Indians in the hope of making a sale.

The man stood waiting quietly by the garden steps. He was young, tall, very thin, and wore the Moslem's wide cotton trousers, collarless shirt and a loose dark waistcoat. As I put the note back into its envelope and looked at him he smiled an ingratiating diffident smile and, shuffling off his slippers, stepped on large bare feet into the verandah and squatted down by my side.

I knew exactly what would be in the square parcel

* *Chiken-wallah*: embroiderer.

that he was already unfastening on the red stone floor. I did not want any nightgowns embroidered with blue and pink flowers, or any table mats. I disliked all such embroidery of patterns learnt from missionaries and a long line of memsahibs, handed down from father to son, from family to family. 'I don't want anything today,' I said, and then remembered that he had undoubtedly paid a few annas to my watchman to be allowed through the gates, perhaps a few more to the servant who had brought the note to me. 'Very well,' I said, though crossly because I had been interrupted in my work, a novel that was not going well, 'let's see what you have there.'

I sat down and watched the narrow pale brown hands set out what he had brought in neat little piles on his cotton sheet at my feet. He had a long gentle bony face, like the face of an antelope, a very long neck with a large Adam's apple, and thick black hair, carefully oiled. Very delicately he laid a child's dress on my knee.

'No, no, there are no children here,' I heard myself say, and at once it was whisked away as if to show that such a sad admission had not even been heard and was replaced by a tablecloth.

'No,' I said again, 'show me some handkerchiefs.' Handkerchiefs were always useful as Christmas presents.

The work was not particularly good. I had seen finer embroidery, but the patterns were more original than usual; they had been finely and carefully drawn by someone with a sure sense of design and a lively imagination. I bought several things that I did not need and gave an order for two dozen handkerchiefs to be monogrammed at four annas a letter.

He smiled again and produced a small shabby book in which I wrote down my order, name and address. I knew without being told that he wanted me to turn the pages and read the other names written there. These were not very many, but some I knew and there were several remarks such as, 'Can strongly recommend this man,' scribbled below them. When I handed the book back to him and saw the look of pleasure, of gentle pride on his face, I was not surprised. He had large brown smiling eyes with too-long lashes, and also an irritating little cough. He packed up his wares slowly. I saw him look round my creeper-hung verandah and out into the green and peaceful garden with what I can only describe as true appreciation and a dreamy delight. I watched him get to his feet and go down the steps and walk reluctantly away. When he reached the hibiscus hedge he stopped and stretched out a hand, then looked round at me for permission. I nodded; he picked one of the scarlet trumpet flowers and put it behind his ear where it looked perfectly in place. Then I went back to my work and forgot all about him.

He was back with my completed order in an incredibly short time. All I could do under that gently appealing gaze was to give him another order and write letters of recommendation to all the friends I could think of. 'I'm in no hurry,' I told him. 'Take your time. I want this work very carefully done.' I saw from the smile he gave me that he knew what I really meant; it was three weeks before I found him standing once more by the steps.

It was cold that morning, I remember, and I told him to come into my sitting-room. I glanced up from the table mats he had brought me to find him examining the room, looking from the carpet to the books and at the flowers in their vases with the same pleasure and interest he had shown in my garden. Then he sat down on the carpet and spread out his cotton cloth. 'I don't want anything today, Rahmin,' I said weakly, knowing it was no use.

That was the beginning of an acquaintance that endured for several years. At first he did not try me too much. He would space his visits carefully. 'Rahmin is here,' my servant would say, and I would leave my work and go out to the verandah where he would be sitting with everything he had to sell invitingly set out. We would talk a little. He would show me tracings of new patterns he had drawn. I would ask about his children and he would admire my cats whose blue eyes fascinated him.

One day I said to him, 'That's a horrid cough. Have you done anything about it?' He looked away at once, murmuring something about being a poor man, about his children. Examining his thin shoulders, hollow cheeks and shining eyes, I said, 'You should go to hospital, but I suppose you won't even if I give you a letter for the doctor sahib?' He shook his head and, sighing, I got up to go to my medicine cupboard. As I gave him cough mixture and cod-liver oil I said, more sharply than I meant, 'It's too stupid! You won't do anything to help yourself.'

At once he shrank into himself; I saw him wilt at my tone as those tiresome sensitive plants do when you touch them; his hands trembled as he hastily packed up his bundle.

He did not come back for a long time and I had begun to worry about him before he reappeared. In my relief at seeing him, thinner than ever but his clothes as clean, his smile as appealing, I wrote down a long order in his little book and gave him a bigger advance than I had done before.

From that day he came more often as if he felt that now there was a bond between us that I would not break. Soon he was a nuisance, a gentle, still oddly welcome, nuisance. Once or twice when my servants said, 'Rahmin has come,' I shook my head and went firmly on with my work. Sometimes he would take the hint, letting several weeks go by before he came again. Sometimes he came back the very next day. Times were hard in Calcutta that year; food was short, prices high. There was much misery everywhere but the continual sight of poverty has a blunting effect; in desperation and helplessness one pulls blinds down over one's eyes, refusing to see or hear any more. I saw, but would not see, that Rahmin was not as he had always been. His clothes were frayed, not always clean, his hair long and dull, his cough harsher and more persistent. It seemed to me sometimes that there was an air of quiet desperation about him. I missed the serenity that I was used to feeling when I saw his smile, yet he never complained or asked anything of me except that I buy what he had to sell and I shrank from asking the questions that I might have asked.

It was raining that last day in July. The rainy season in Calcutta is unhealthy and depressing, rain and heat together being trying on the nerves. All morning I had sat at my desk sweating and cross, struggling to work. 'Not today,' I said to my servant, 'tell him to go away.'

When I looked up again Rahmin was in the room. He stood with his bundle in his hand, silently willing me to realise that he was there. The edges of his cotton trousers were soaked, his bare feet glistened; his hair, unoiled and dull, hung over his forehead. He looked exasperatingly abject and dirty and made no attempt to smile at me. Through the open doorway behind him I could see his large black umbrella propped against one of the verandah pillars.

The time had come to make some kind of stand, I told

myself, hardening my heart; there was a limit. 'I'm not buying anything today, Rahmin,' I said, 'and it's no use asking me for another advance. It's only a week since you came. Go away, I'm busy.' I picked up my pencil again.

After a moment's silence I knew that he had not gone. 'Go away,' I repeated, 'go and pester someone else.'

I heard a long sigh, then a faint rustle and movement. Out of the corner of my eye I saw a brown hand lay something down on my desk.

'I tell you, I'm not buying anything,' I said, losing my temper.

A gentle voice interrupted me. 'Not to buy. A present.'

The words took some time to penetrate. When I laid my pencil down and looked up, the room was empty. On the desk lay two folded traycloths, hemstitched, embroidered. I took them up, looking at the myriads of small careful stitches and then round the room.

My house is a modest house, small, a little damp, rather shabby and by some standards even primitive, but, as I looked across the verandah and out into the garden, it became an enormous palace filled with unattainable riches, shot with gold, soft with unimaginable comfort. I was looking at it and at myself with Rahmin's eyes.

Still holding the traycloths, I rushed out of the room into the rain and across the drive. I flung the gates open and looked up and down the road. The road was thronged as it always was. I ran a little way along it, pushing through the people, dodging the cars and buses, but I could see no sign of Rahmin.

'He will come back,' I told myself, as I went back into the house. 'He will be back in a day or two with his bundle and then I will buy everything in it, even if it ruins me,' but Rahmin did not come back in a day or two, or ever.

I made enquiries, questioned my friends. I tried to find him, but Rahmin had gone. I never saw him again except in my mind, where he remains as a small and shameful scar.

Monkey

I first saw the monkey one early monsoon morning in the garden. It sat on the steps that went down to the pool where the water-lily leaves shone in the sunlight after the night's rain. In the rainy season this Calcutta garden was too green, too luxuriant. That morning it smelt like a jungle of rotting greenness, flowers and mud, also of the open drain between the nine-foot-high garden walls and the busy road beyond them.

We were used to finding strange creatures in both garden and house: insects galore, lizards of all sizes from the huge iguana that lived in one of the drains to the little house lizards on the bedroom ceiling, bats, toads, frogs. When the rains were heavy and the garden flooded, I had even found fish wriggling on the lawn. Snakes often came indoors trying to find somewhere solid and dry in their soaked world and were tolerated, if not exactly welcomed, unless they were poisonous which they seldom were. I had seen wild monkeys, both the small brown rhesus and the large languars, in the trees beyond the lawn, but a tame monkey, one that showed no fear of me, was an innovation. I was delighted. I planned to keep it if no one claimed it. It could join the dogs waiting on the drive behind me, and the cats, invisible that morning and probably sunning themselves on the flat roof.

I went into the house to fetch a banana and when I came back the monkey was still there, sitting with its hands on its knees. It lifted its head as I approached; its eyes were brown but cold; I noticed its neat ears flat on its skull and the smooth crown of its head, then saw it had a piece of broken-off string round its neck. 'So you do belong to somebody,' I told it.

When it saw the banana, it stood up on its hind legs and held up a grey-palmed hand. I expected it to chatter at me but it made no sound. It did not snatch but took the fruit, sat down again, and removed the peel so delicately and carefully with its small fingers that I was charmed. This was no common rhesus monkey; it was gold-brown all over with a paler chest and belly and a very long tail. I thought that I had never seen such a pretty little monkey before. It ate fastidiously, contemplating the hibiscus and plumbago bushes as it did so, taking no more notice of me.

A whistle sounded from the road, a high shrill human whistle that came clearly to us through the sound of traffic. I started. The monkey turned its head. It looked up at me as it stuffed the last of the banana into its cheek, a cold impersonal look. Then it stood up, seized my leg in both hands, bit me hard on the calf, and was up a creeper, over the wall, and down into the road before I could even feel astonished or pained.

The bite was not very deep. I examined it in the bathroom, applied iodine and a bandage, and then, shocked but not surprised at such ingratitude, such a return for my hospitality, I went back to the garden. Monkeys will be monkeys, was what I thought, and, that's that.

But that was only the beginning.

The car, as usual, brought my husband, Roland, back from the city; our high shabby green-painted gates opened to admit it and closed again. We had friends to see us that evening; the before-dinner drinks were set out on the back verandah. This broad verandah, overhung with creepers between its square pillars, looked out at the garden and was the main sitting-room of the house. It had large comfortable upholstered chairs, rugs and two standard lamps as well as pots of flowers, an aviary and a low built-in concrete and glass aquarium for my tropical fish. I had bathed and changed and was prepared for a leisurely and pleasant evening but I had made the mistake of wearing a short skirt. The bandage was noticed at once, and the fuss that was to last for days began.

'A monkey? What monkey?'

'How often have I told you not to touch strange animals.' Roland was cross.

'A monkey's bite is very dangerous.'

'Rabies. Have you thought of rabies?'

In my life in India I had endured the full course of anti-rabies injections five times, the first time as a four-year-old child when I was bitten by a mad dog on a tea-plantation in Assam. The injections are very painful, given every day into the stomach wall for fourteen days. Six months before my encounter with the monkey, I had gone through it all again although, as far as I knew, I had not touched my friend's spaniel that died of the disease. I had no intention of repeating the experience so soon.

'It was a tame monkey,' I protested. 'Perfectly healthy,' but my protests were brushed aside and to save the evening's peace I agreed to go to the doctor next day.

The doctor advised the full course of injections, as he was bound to do. 'You know the risk,' he said. 'You would have to wait for six months after this bite before you could be certain you were safe. That's a long time. Surely it's worth the bother just to set your mind at rest?'

To me it was not. My stomach ached at the thought. I was busy and did not want to drive into the city every day. I was certain that there was nothing wrong with the monkey, and finally the doctor said, 'Well then, if you will be so obstinate you must find that monkey, then see it every day. If it's alive and well at the end of five days, or say a week to be sure, you can forget all about it.'

On my way home I made some enquiries in the bazaar that lay on each side of the road between the tram depot and my house.

My one-storeyed, flat-roofed house, hidden behind its garden walls from the road that went from Calcutta, six miles away, out to the open countryside, was one of a small residential estate whose old buildings and old green gardens were now an oasis in the spreading new concrete suburbs that had sprung up so quickly after the war. The houses and their grounds had long ago belonged to a nawab who had housed his harem, dancing-girls, state carriages, horses and armed guard there. Our house was the smallest and the last; it had once been the grain store.

No one in the bazaar could, or would, tell me anything about the monkey so when I reached home I sent for our watchman, Gunga Ram, a squat elderly Gurkha. He wore khaki shorts and a bush-jacket, a round black hat and sometimes boots and puttees. He had nothing to do all day but open and shut the gate and keep intruders away. At night, after making his rounds, he slept peacefully in his blankets on the front verandah, but his presence was enough to keep burglars away. He was resourceful and conceited so I sent him out to succeed where I had failed.

In a few hours I learned that the monkey belonged to a

Bengali gentleman called Dey who lived two miles further down the road. The monkey was his children's pet, greatly loved and absolutely harmless. Every day for fresh air and exercise, it accompanied Mr Dey's servant to the bazaar when he bicycled there to buy fresh provisions. Always it rode before him on the handlebars, safely attached by a piece of string. If by any chance it disappeared for a few minutes it always answered the servant's whistle. Everyone in the bazaar knew the monkey. Now that Gunga Ram came to think of it, he had often seen it going by, with a can of milk slung from the handlebars in front of it.

'If you persist in going on with this silliness,' Roland told me, 'you must go and see Mr Dey.'

Mr Dey, a stout young man wearing a white muslin shirt and *dhoti*, was polite but suspicious. He did not ask me into his new concrete bungalow but came out on to the front steps, followed by several children. The monkey, carried by the servant, was produced and at once the children set up a wail; never, never, had it bitten anyone and was adored by all. When it was understood that I was not there to complain, in spite of the bandage on my leg, quiet was restored and Mr Dey, ordering the children back into the house, agreed readily that my watchman should bicycle over every day, 'just to see that the monkey was well'.

I suggested that perhaps it would be easier if his servant, as he passed out house every day, brought the monkey in to see me on his way to or from the bazaar, but Mr Dey would have none of this. The monkey would not be allowed out again, he wanted no more trouble. 'Glad to oblige,' he said kindly. 'No harm, no harm,' and waved goodbye to me from the steps.

For two days all was well. Each evening Gunga Ram reported that the monkey was alive and in good health.

On the third evening he said calmly that the monkey had gone.

'Gone? Where?'

Gunga Ram's flat gold wrinkled face grimaced, as it always did if he had any bad news to tell. Mr Dey had given the monkey away, he said. The Bengali was tired of the trouble the monkey was causing and he did not want a strange hill-man coming to his house every day. It was not true that the monkey had never bitten anyone. It bit the children frequently and had once nearly taken the finger off a shopkeeper in the bazaar. Mr Dey, it seemed, had refused to say where the monkey had gone but, being resourceful, Gunga Ram had gone round to the back of the bungalow where the servant admitted that his master had presented it to the Chirria-khana, the Bird-house, the Indian's name for the Calcutta Zoo.

Gunga Ram left the room saluting, pleased with himself as he always was.

'Sent to the zoo,' said Roland. 'That's a likely tale. Dey has had that monkey put down. Now you will have to give in. Begin the injections tomorrow and let's have some peace,' but next morning I went to the zoo.

It was a pleasant place – for human beings – with its ornamental lakes covered with wild duck, its flowering trees that shaded the animal houses, its lawns and winding paths. I had often been there to see the collection of pheasants, which was the Superintendent's pride. I knew the Superintendent who had been sympathetic and helpful when I went to him with questions about birds and animals, and in return I had been able to give him a pair of rare Tragopan birds for his collection. After I had clicked through the turnstiles, paying my two annas, I went straight to his office, only to find that he was away and not expected back for three days.

Two clerks looked up the records for me. Mr Dey had given the monkey to the zoo, the entry was there with Mr Dey's name and address. I tried to explain my predicament and was directed to the monkey house where I was told I would find the keeper.

The monkey house, a large yellow building among the trees, was impossible to miss because of the monkey sounds and smells coming from it. Hundreds of monkeys, or so it seemed to me, looked down at me from behind the bars and hundreds of small hands were stretched out for the monkey nuts I had neglected to buy at the gates. The break in the rains persisted and the whole world sweated and steamed; I stood there feeling helpless and foolish. The monkey smell was stronger every minute but I gathered up my determination and went inside the building where at least it was cooler. There was no sign of a keeper, but I found a man sweeping down the stone floor with a brush and a bucket of disinfectant. I repeated my story, gave him a rupee, and was taken at once to a huge cage at the far end of the building. The sweeper knew all about the monkey, he said. It was in there, playing with its fellows. There it was, at the top, hanging on to that swing.

I had been sure that I would recognise the monkey, but one small brown monkey is very like another. There must have been at least thirty, silhouetted against the sunlit green beyond their bars. They were playing, squabbling, flinging themselves from swing to swing, changing places bewilderingly, or sitting in rows along the branches of the dead tree provided for them. They all looked alike to me.

'Are you sure?' I asked.

'Without a doubt,' he said soothingly. 'Or perhaps it's that one over there in the corner.'

I went away after he had assured me that all the monkeys in the building were in good health. It was now five days since I had been bitten. I drove home thoughtfully. Rabies is always fatal, and a most unpleasant way to die but, I decided, I would wait a few more days until the Superintendent came back.

The next day I was at the zoo again, with Gunga Ram and a bag of monkey nuts. He made no pretence of recognising the monkey but he found a keeper, a kindly old man in a khaki uniform who told me he knew all that was to be known about monkeys. Had he not worked here for twenty years? Unfortunately he could not help me; he had only come back on duty that morning after his holiday and he knew nothing about my monkey. He looked at me pityingly but answered my searching questions as to the health of the monkeys with patience. Not one was ailing, it seemed. Yes, he would certainly know if one was even a little off its feed. That one, sitting by itself? No, there was nothing wrong with it. Yes, he would make enquiries and be here on this very spot, if I wished it, tomorrow morning. Followed by a grinning Gunga Ram and shrieks of monkey laughter, I left the building.

In the following days the monkeys in that cage came to know me well. They swarmed down the bars to meet me and my monkey nuts when I appeared. Busy as I was, I visited them morning and evening, splashing to them through the rain which had started again, ignoring comments at home that it would surely save time and bother to visit the doctor once every day. I was still positive that there had been nothing wrong with my monkey, except an unpleasant character, but must admit I woke in the night feeling doubtful, faintly uneasy; I made myself turn over and go to sleep again and each morning found me as determined as ever; I was not going to endure those injections again. Both keeper and sweeper, kept attentive by good tips, humoured me and stood beside me while I did my best to examine each monkey. Then at last, late one day, the Superintendent came back.

I saw him, a tall middle-aged man in white drill trousers and a white shirt, standing in the doorway of his office as, through the rain, I passed once more round the turnstiles. He listened to my story, then called to one of his clerks. A file was brought and examined; a flood of Bengali followed, too fast and angry for me to understand. The clerk crept away, but when Mr Lahiri turned to me he was smiling.

'Come with me,' he said.

As we went towards the monkey house under our umbrellas he said gently, 'You should have asked for my assistant. He could have saved you some trouble and much anxiety, I think? He has been here all the time.'

'Your clerks never told me.'

He shrugged his shoulders. 'Perhaps they did not understand you very well, or perhaps they thought it no business of theirs; they are only clerks. My assistant would have told you that directly it arrived at the zoo this monkey was quarantined, kept apart from the rest for a few days to make sure of its health, as all new arrivals are. It was let out this morning, a little early for a special reason.'

I stood still on the path. 'Do you mean to tell me that the monkey was never in that cage?' I cried. 'But the sweeper, not to mention the keeper?'

He shrugged his shoulders again and said apologetically, 'They are poor men and doubtless the sweeper did not know when you first asked him. As for the keeper, well, I expect that in your anxiety you were a little too generous with your rupees, but let us say that perhaps he did not understand you either.'

He walked on and I hurried after him, swallowing my wrath. 'How is the monkey?' I asked.

'It's in the best of health, as you will see for yourself in a moment,' he said. I saw that he was smiling broadly. As we walked into the big damp odorous and only too familiar monkey house, he laughed outright.

Both keeper and sweeper were waiting as usual for me at the far end of the building; at the sight of the Superintendent they vanished abruptly through the end door.

'Walk quietly,' the Superintendent warned me as he led the way down a side aisle that ended in a line of small and mostly empty cages. Over one a tarpaulin had been fixed; this he lifted gently. 'Monkeys take time to get acquainted,' he said softly, 'and like human beings prefer privacy at times.'

There were two small brown monkeys in the cage which was furnished with a leafy branch and a heap of straw. They sat in opposite corners and they looked exactly alike, exactly like my monkey.

'We should be grateful to you,' the Superintendent said. 'You see, for some time we have had a female of this rather rare species, a native of Nicobar, but until a week ago had been unable to procure a healthy full-grown male. How this one came into Mr Dey's possession I have yet to find out but, thanks to you, there it is, a fine specimen. We hope for a happy and fruitful union before long.'

He looked fondly at the inhabitants of the honeymoon

cage and then adjusted the tarpaulin carefully and turned to me.

'All's well that ends well,' he said, beaming down at me. 'A happy ending to your story.'

Sister Malone and
the Obstinate Man

Sister Malone had an extraordinary capacity for faith. She was in charge of the Out-Patients in the Elizabeth Scott Memorial Hospital for Women and Children, in a suburb of Calcutta, run by the Anglican order to which she belonged. She needed her faith; terrible things passed under her hands.

All sorts of patients came in all sorts of vehicles, rickshaws, curtained or uncurtained, hired carriages that had shutters to close them – they looked like boxes on wheels; a taxi with an accident case lying on the floor so that the blood should not soil the cushions, perhaps a case that the taxi itself had run over – it was astonishing how often taxis did run over patients. A few came pillion on a bicycle; some could walk and some were carried; there were fathers carrying children, mothers carrying children, small children carrying smaller children. Sometimes whole families brought one patient; servants of the rich brought their charges, or their mistress, or brought themselves. There were Hindu women in purdah, Moslem women in *burkas*, white coverings like tents that hid them from their heads to the ground, and hill women walking free as did the beggar women. There were high-caste Brahmins and untouchables; all colours of skin, dark, brown, pale; and all sorts of flesh, soft, pampered, thin, withered, sweet, ill-treated.

There were diseased women, diseased children, burned children; even more often there were tubercular children; deep and dreadful tubercular abscesses on breasts and groins and armpits were common. There was a great deal of ophthalmia and rickets and scabies, cases of leprosy and poisoning and fevers; there were broken bones made septic by neglect or wounds treated with dung and oozing pus. There were bites from rabid dogs and sometimes bites from human beings and, like a repeated chorus, always, burns and tuberculosis. This was not the result of famine or of war, this was everyday, an everyday average in one of the departments of one of the hospitals in the city, an everyday sample of its pain and poverty and indifference and the misuse of its human beings. Sister Malone certainly needed that extraordinary faith.

Most of the sisters who were detailed to help her asked to be transferred after a few months; they became haunted and could not sleep. Sister Malone had worked here for seven years. 'Sister, how can you? I . . . you . . . I . . . I cannot bear it, Sister.'

'You must have faith,' said Sister Malone, and she quoted, as she had quoted a hundred hundred times: ' "And now abideth faith, hope and love, these three." ' She paused, gazing through the thick lenses of her glasses that made her look a little blind. 'God forgive me for differing,' said Sister Malone, 'but you know, dear, the greatest to me is faith.' Then a question, a little persistent question, sometimes reared its head: was Sister Malone lacking a little in love, a little unsympathetic? Surely not. She was so splendid with the patients, though there was one small sign that no one noticed; the patients called her Didi – 'Sister'; she spoke of them as 'they', a race apart. 'If only,' she said – and she said this continually – 'if only they could have a little faith for themselves!'

She tried to give it to them. In the corner of the treatment room there was a shelf on which lay paper-covered gospels translated into Hindi, Bengali, Urdu, and Gurkhali. Sister Malone gave one to every patient. She walked sincerely in what she believed to be the footsteps of Christ. 'It is seeing so much eye-trouble and lepers', said Sister Malone, 'that makes it so very vivid. Of course Our Lord knew that lepers are not nearly as infectious as is commonly thought. People are so mistaken about lepers,' said Sister Malone earnestly. 'I have always thought it a pity to use the word "unclean". I have known some quite clean lepers. Think of it, dear,' she said wistfully, 'He put out His hand and touched them and made them whole. So quick! Here it is such a slow, slow business. But of course,' she said and sighed, 'they need to have faith.'

Sister Malone was a small firm flat woman. Her hands probably knew more of actual India, had probed it more deeply, than any politician's brain. These implements – yes, implements, because the dictionary definition of 'implement' is 'whatever may fill up or supply a want' and that was a good description of Sister Malone's hands – these implements were small and flat and firm; they needed to be firm.

At eight o'clock one blinding white-hot morning in June, just before the break of the rains, Sister Malone, Sister Shelley, and Sister Latch walked into the treatment room. Over their white habits, black girdles and the ebony crucifixes on their breasts they put on aprons; the crosses showed through the bibs. They turned up their sleeves and went across to the sink, where the tap ran perpetually, to scrub their hands, nails, wrists, and forearms, and afterwards immerse them in a basin of water and disinfectant.

Sister Shelley and Sister Latch were the two nuns detailed to help in the treatment room at that time. Sister Shelley was pale, her face drawn and sensitive between the bands of her coif; her eyes looked as if she had a headache. Sister Latch was newly out from home. Her steps were firm and certain; her pink face was made pinker by the heat; her body, well fed, solid, was already sweating through her clothes. She was cheerful, observant, sensible and interested. It was her first morning with the Out-Patients.

Through the window, as she scrubbed her hands, she noticed two little green parakeets tumbling in a gul-mohr tree. She would have liked to draw the other sisters' attention to them but she did not dare.

The Out-Patients was divided into the doctor's room, the waiting-hall, the dispensary, and the treatment room, which had a small examination room leading off it. The patients waited in the hall, which was furnished only with pictures; they sat in rows on the floor. Each went to the doctor in turn and then, with their tickets in their hands, were admitted to the dispensary for free medicine, or to the treatment room for dressings, examination, slight operations, or emergency treatment. 'You let no one in without a ticket,' said Sister Malone to Sister Latch, 'and you treat no one unless the ticket bears today's date and the doctor's signature. You can let the first two in.'

Sister Latch went eagerly. There was already a crowd and it pressed round the door, a collection of dark faces, clothes and rags and nakedness and smells. Sister Latch held up two fingers and cried, 'Two,' in her new Bengali, but seven edged past her into the room.

'It's all right,' said Sister Shelley in her even, toneless voice. 'There are only two. The others are relations,' and she set to work.

The first case was nothing remarkable, a septic ear; a woman of the sweeper class sat herself down on a stool and, clasping her ankles until she was bent almost double, inclined her head to her shoulder so that Sister Shelley could conveniently clean her ear. Sister Malone was poulticing, in a woman's armpit, an abscess which had been opened the day before.

The next two patients came, and then another, an old woman. 'You can attend to her,' said Sister Shelley to Sister Latch. 'She is an old case and knows what to do.' Sister Latch went slowly up to the woman. She was a crone, wound in a meagre grey-white cotton sari that showed her naked waist and withered filthy breasts; her head was shaved and her feet were bare. She sat down on a stool and began to unwind an enormous, dirty bandage on her thumb.

'Don't do that,' said Sister Latch. 'Let me.'

'*Nahin*, baba,' said the old woman, unwinding steadily, 'you fetch the bowl for it to soak in.'

Sister Latch had not been called 'child' before. A little piqued, she looked round. 'That is the bowl,' said the old woman, pointing to a kidney-dish on the table. 'The hot water is there, and there is the medicine.' She had come to the last of the bandage and she shut her eyes. 'You can pull it off,' she said. 'It makes me sick.'

Sister Latch pulled, and a tremor shook her that seemed to open a fissure from her knees through her stomach to her heart. The thumb was a stump, swollen, gangrened. 'It – it makes me sick, too,' said poor Sister Latch, and ran out.

When she came back the thumb was soaking and Sister Shelley was preparing the dressing. 'She is a maidservant in a rich house,' said Sister Shelley without emotion, 'and they make her go on working, scouring cooking-pots and washing up; with the thumb continually in water, of course it cannot heal.'

Sister Latch was dumb with indignation and pity.

At that moment Sister Malone came bustling back. 'Ah, Tarala!' she said to the old woman in Bengali. 'Well, how's your disgraceful thumb?' She took it gently from the bath. 'Ah, it's better!' She examined it. 'It *is* better. It actually is. Look, Sisters, do you see how it's beginning to slough off here? Isn't that wonderful? Give me the scissors. Now the dressing, Sister, quickly.' Her fingers wound on the bandage swiftly and steadily. She finished and lifted the hand and put it in the bosom of the sari. 'There, that's beautiful,' she said, and the old woman crept out, still seared with pain but comforted.

'But *how* can it heal?' asked Sister Latch, with tears in her sympathetic eyes. 'What is the use?'

'We must hope for the best,' said Sister Malone.

Sister Shelley was silent.

'We must temper our work with faith,' said Sister Malone, emptying the kidney-dish. Steeped in ritual and reality, Sister Malone's words were often accidentally beautiful. 'We must have faith for them, Sister Latch, dear. Sister Shelley, this child is for operation.' She put a piece of brown paper under the child's dusty feet as he lay on the table. He began to scream as Sister Shelley took his hands.

The abscess on his forehead was like a rhinoceros horn; he was a dark little boy, and the skin round the abscess was stretched and strained with colours of olive-green and

50

fig-purple. His eyes rolled with fright, showing the whites, and the muscles of his stomach were drawn in and tensed into the shape of a cave under his ribs. He screamed in short, shrill screams as the doctor came in.

Suddenly Sister Shelley began to scream as well. She was holding the boy's hands out of the way while Sister Malone cleaned his forehead, and now she beat them on the table. 'Stop that noise!' she shrieked. 'Stop that! Stop! Stop that noise!'

Sister Malone knocked her hands away, spun her round by the shoulders and marched her outside, then came in quickly and shut the doors. 'Take her place, Sister Latch,' she said curtly. 'The doctor is here.'

'But – no anaesthetic?' asked Sister Latch.

'There's no money for anaesthetics for a small thing like this,' said Sister Malone sadly. 'Never mind,' she added firmly. 'It is over in a minute.'

The morning went on growing steadily hotter, the smells steadily stronger, the light more blindingly white. The heat in the treatment room was intense, and both sisters were wet, their hands clammy. In half an hour Sister Shelley, made curiously empty and blank by her tears, came back. Sister Malone said nothing. The patients came in until Sister Latch lost count of them; the wounds, the sores, disease and shame were shown; the room echoed with cries, screams, tears – rivers of tears, thought Sister Latch.

Then, in the middle of the hubbub, quiet descended.

A car had driven up, a large car, and from it two young men had jumped down, calling for a stretcher. They were well-dressed young Hindus in white, and between them they lifted from the car something small and fragile and very still, wrapped in vivid violet and green. Sister Latch saw a fall of long black hair.

The stretcher was brought straight into the treatment room, and the girl was lifted from it to the table. She lay inert, with the brilliant colours heaped round her. Her face was a pale oval turned up to the ceiling, her mouth white-brown, her nostrils wide as if they were stamped with fright, and her eyes open, glazed, the pupils enormous. Her hair hung to the floor and she was very young. 'Seventeen?' asked Sister Latch. 'Or sixteen? How beautiful she is.' She looked again and cried, 'Sister, she's dead.'

'She is breathing,' said Sister Malone. Her flat little hand was spread on the girl's heart.

One of the young men was terribly unnerved. Sister Latch wondered if he were the husband. He shivered as he stood waiting by the table. 'She t-took her l-life,' he said.

The other man, darker, stronger, said sternly, 'Be quiet.'

'And why? Why?' asked Sister Malone's eyes, but she said evenly, 'Well, she didn't succeed. She is breathing.'

'You th-think th-there is – hope?'

'There is always hope', said Sister Malone, 'while there is breath.'

Then the doctor and orderlies came in with pails and the stomach-pump and the young men were sent out of the room. Sister Shelley went to the window and stood there with her back to everyone; Sister Malone, after a glance at her, let her stand. 'You will have to help me,' said Sister Malone to Sister Latch. 'Be strong.'

'But – only tell me what it is *about*. I don't understand,' cried Sister Latch, quite out of herself. 'I don't understand.'

'She has poisoned herself,' said Sister Malone. 'Opium poisoning. Look at her eyes.'

'But why?' cried Sister Latch again. 'Why? She's so young. So beautiful. Why should she?'

'It – is best not to be too curious.'

'Yes,' said Sister Shelley suddenly, still with her back to them, 'don't ask. Don't understand. Only try and drag her back – for more.'

After a time the doctor paused; bent; waited another minute; stood up and slowly, still carefully, began to withdraw the tube.

'No!' said Sister Malone, her hands still busy.

'Yes,' said the doctor, and the last of the hideous tube came from the girl's mouth. He wiped her chin, gently closed her mouth and drew down the lids, but the mouth would not stay closed; it dropped open in an O that looked childish and dismayed, contradicting the sternness of the face and sealed lids.

'Snuffed out,' said Sister Malone, as she stood up, gently put the draperies back and looked down on the girl's shut face. 'They have nothing to sustain them,' said Sister Malone, 'nothing at all.'

Sister Latch began to cry quietly. The young men came in and carried the girl away and, from the window, the sisters saw the car drive away, with a last sight of violet and green on the back seat. A tear slid down Sister Latch's cheek. 'Forgive me,' she said but no one answered; her tears slid unnoticed into that great river of tears. 'Forgive me,' said Sister Latch, 'she wore . . . exactly the same green . . . as those little parrots.'

She stood in tears; Sister Shelley seemed chiselled in stone, but Sister Malone was tidying up the room for the next patients. 'Nothing to sustain them,' said Sister Malone and sighed.

At the very end of the morning, when they had finished and taken off their aprons, an old man came into the waiting-hall from the doctor's room. He moved slowly and led a small girl by the wrist; he held his ticket uncertainly between his finger and thumb as if he did not know what to do with it.

'Another!' said Sister Shelley. 'It's too late.'

'No,' said Sister Malone with her faithful exactness. 'It wants one minute to one o'clock, when we should stop,' and she took the paper. 'It is nothing,' she said, 'only stitches to be taken out of a cut on the child's lip. I remember her now. You may go, Sisters. It won't take me five minutes.'

Sister Malone was left with the man and the child.

As she lifted the scissors from the steriliser with the forceps she caught his gaze fixed on her and she saw that he was not old, only emaciated until his flesh had sunken in. His skin was a curious dead grey-brown.

'You are ill,' said Sister Malone.

'I am ill,' the man agreed, his voice calm.

Sister Malone turned the little girl to the light. The child began to whimper and the man to plead with her in a voice quite different from the one he had used when he had spoken of himself. 'She will not hurt you. *Nahin. Nahin. Nahin.*'

'Of course I will not hurt you if you stand still,' said Sister Malone to the child. 'Hold her shoulders.'

The child gave two cries as the stitches came out, but she did not move, though the tears ran from her eyes and the sweat poured off the man. When it was over and he could release his hands he staggered. Sister Malone thought he would have fallen if she had not caught him and helped him to a stool. His arm was burning.

'You have fever,' said Sister Malone.

'I continually have fever,' said the man.

'What is it you have?'

'God knows,' he answered but as if he were satisfied, not wondering.

'You don't know? But you are very ill. Haven't you seen the doctor?'

'No.'

'Then you must come with me at once,' said Sister Malone energetically. 'I will take you to the doctor.'

'I do not need a doctor.'

'But – how can we know what to do for you? How can you know?'

'I do not need to know.'

'But you should have medicine – treatment.'

He smiled. 'I have my medicine.'

His smile was so peculiarly calm that it made Sister Malone pause. She looked at him silently, searchingly. He smiled again and opened the front of his shirt and showed her where, round his neck, hung a silver charm on a red thread of the sort she saw every day and all day long round the necks of men and women and children. He held it and turned his face upwards, and his eyes. 'My medicine,' he said. 'God.'

Sister Malone suddenly flushed. 'That is absurd,' she said. 'You will die.'

'If I die I am happy.'

'But, man!' cried Sister Malone. 'You mean you will give yourself up without a struggle?'

'Why should I struggle?'

'Come with me to the doctor.'

'No.'

'That's sheer senseless obstinacy,' cried Sister Malone. 'If you won't come, let me fetch him to you.'

'No.'

'Obstinate! Obstinate!' Her eyes behind her glasses

looked bewildered and even more blind. 'You came for the child,' she said, 'then why not for yourself?'

'She is too young to choose her path. I have chosen.' There was a silence. 'Come, Jaya,' he said gently, 'greet the Sister Sahib and we shall go.'

'Wait. Wait one minute. If you won't listen to me, let the doctor talk to you. He is wise and good. Let him talk to you.'

She had barred his way and the man seemed to grow more dignified and a little stern. 'Let me go,' he said. 'I have told you. I need nothing. I have everything. I have God.'

Sister Malone, left alone, was furious as she washed her hands; her face was red and her glasses glittered. 'Mumbo-jumbo!' she said furiously as she turned the tap off. 'Mumbo-jumbo! Heavens! What an obstinate man!'

The Grey Budgerigar

The aviary was in Tollygunj, a leafy, flowery and elegant suburb of Calcutta.

The grey budgerigar was not young. Her beak was thick and pale, but she had a bright kind black eye and soft smoky grey feathers. When she was in the little cage she gaily turned somersaults in each corner to show that there was plenty of life in the old girl yet.

The grey budgerigar was brought to be a solution to our pale blue widower whose little yellow wife had died the week before in spite of his care and devotion, his passionate protection. She broke her beak on the wire and could not feed herself but he fed her assiduously, covering her broken uplifted mouth with seed. When she was dead he stood over her calling out, demanding to know where she had gone. For a long time he hated us because he saw us carrying her away.

The grey budgerigar was soon at home, flying about the aviary, eating busily, and trying to put the lovebirds in their proper places. Her husband was kind and thoughtful but not enthusiastic. Perhaps he did not like her tough ways of standing up to the lovebirds or perhaps he found her too different, too energetic, too *grey* after his mourned yellow one.

The wicked lovebirds, one blue-black, the other green,

red and gold but both with large sharp hooked beaks of iron strength, gave the grey budgerigar no mercy. If only she had been content to fly away from them, to give up the nesting boxes to them, all might have been well, but no – she fought back and defied them; she wanted a nice box to put her future eggs in. Soon her beak, too, was broken off short to her nose showing her tongue. The blue husband was wounded in the breast and lost a toe. The battle was lost and the evil lovebirds – misnamed – strutted and flaunted and hung upside down from their swing, once more in undisputed possession of their world.

Put in their little cage, the budgerigars lived for a short time, looking out through the wires at the green garden. He was sorry and kind, very kind, but he did not try to feed this wife. She held up her broken face to him but he only made kind noises and sidled away. She tried hard to feed, spending hours picking up the seeds that she could not break; though her round pale brown tongue lifted up the seeds, she could not swallow them. When we held her in our hands she did not struggle and allowed the drops of milk to slide down her throat although they did no good, no good at all.

Astonishingly, the grey budgerigar rallied; we thought she was eating the crushed seed we gave her but after two days she was a ball of ruffled feathers on the perch, with only one eye showing, an eye that was black and bright no longer. Then we knew that she would die.

Her blue husband stayed beside her all day, looking down at the green and sunny garden where the hibiscus swung in the wind and the happy free birds played in the trees. He ate and drank for himself and then returned to the perch to sit by her. Sometimes he crowed a little or chirped a few notes. At night she crept close to him and slept with her head on his shoulder. He kept his beautiful round white and blue head over her and they slept all night with their heads touching.

The grey budgerigar still struggled on. Then she fell with a whirl of wings on to the floor but was soon back on the perch. She tried to eat lying on the plate with her forehead on the seeds. At five o'clock, when the sun was warmly gold in the garden, the afternoon breezy and bright with scarlet flowers moving against the sky, she fell for the last time and died.

The tough gay thread of her courage, the bird spirit, the bird life, the bird 'being', was there in the cage, there in the last look of the black eye, and then there no longer; in the sunny happy garden was no shadow, no momentary paling of the sunlight, no stillness for a second of the flowers.

Children of Aloysius

'The old woman you want for your film', said the voice over the telephone, 'is at the handkerchief counter of the Charitable Working Women's Guild.'

It was a woman's voice, charming, cultured and assured . . . one of the Committee of the Guild perhaps, thought Rhea. 'I thought I should tell you,' said the lady and rang off.

Rhea Stormant, in charge of casting, had had many such calls; all Calcutta knew that the Universal Film Corporation was looking for an elderly Eurasian woman to play the part of Nan, the children's nurse, in the film they had come to India to make. There were so many candidates that sometimes Rhea thought that everyone in this teeming hungry polyglot city wanted to be in the film; she was besieged with letters, telephone calls, pleas for interviews. The lure – American money, publicity, glamour – is the same all over the world, she thought wearily; she was growing very weary. Rhea was waylaid in the street, in shops, in houses; every time she came into the office, it was full; at the last audition there had been more than five hundred women, old and young, black, brown, white and yellow; she was beginning to see faces in her dreams, none of them the right one.

'Couldn't you use Mooni?' she asked Valentine, the director. Mooni was Monisha Thakur, an elderly Indian star.

'I don't want to use professionals,' said Valentine, the famous young Valentine Morley.

'Why not?' Rhea had been exasperated.

'Because I want the truth and simplicity of these people.' Rhea was beginning to be tired of truth and simplicity; it was true that the Indian parts had been easy; they had found boatmen, fishermen, dancers, musicians, farmers, workers, servants, unselfconscious and innately graceful, but the story needed European children, and she had had a long and difficult hunt among the children of the local residents before they found some of whom Valentine approved. 'And *still* you have no Nan,' said Valentine.

'In ten days we go on the floor.' Mr Thunberger was the producer. 'Ten days! Ten days! Mooni is expensive but we think she's good publicity.' Mr Thunberger, like royalty, always said 'we'. 'Val, you will have to settle for Mooni.'

'I won't use Mooni,' and, for the hundredth time he described his idea of Nan. 'Nan is a poor little Eurasian. She must be dark to show up the fairness of the children. She must speak in that sing-song Eurasian way. She must show the marks of toil and patience and she must be humble and noble.'

'But Eurasians are not humble and noble.' Rhea was in despair. 'They are usually conceited and scrubby. Oh, Val! Be practical. There *isn't* a real Nan.'

'There is. Go and find her,' said Valentine. Rhea had sat down at her desk when the telephone rang. It will be another wild goose chase, she thought as she picked up her bag, but I had better go. She called a taxi and set off to find the Working Women's Guild.

It was in one of Calcutta's labyrinthine streets of old decaying wide-balconied and creepered houses that swarm with poor whites, Eurasians and Chinese.

Rhea had to leave the taxi and walk past overflowing dustbins and gutters that stank until she came to a noticeboard over an arched gateway, Working Women's Guild. Inside was a courtyard where women sat sewing at trestle tables. There were Armenians with, even in their unwieldy middle-age, a bloom of skin and beautiful eyes; there were little withered-up Chinese, Christian Madrassi Indians in saris and every kind of Eurasian, some so poor and old that they wore the missionary Mother Hubbard dresses. Rhea's eye, trained by Valentine, travelled carefully over them; there was no possible Nan there so she passed them and went in.

The ground floor of the house was a showroom for lace, fine embroidery, table linen and baby dresses all exquisitely made. Rhea touched the cobweb fineness of a dress in lawn and lace and thought, with a pang, of the poor dark fingers that had sewn it. Perhaps I can give one poor soul a chance, she thought, a little money, a glimpse of life. A big slipshod woman came up to her.

'Could I see the Superintendent?' asked Rhea.

'I am the Superintendent.'

'Could I see some handkerchiefs?'

'Handkerchiefs?' said the Superintendent vaguely. 'Ah!' Her face cleared. 'You want Philomena Francis.'

She took Rhea to a glassed-in counter where a little woman came and spread before Rhea some squares of linen, fine with hemstitching and lace. 'Please to choose.' She spoke in a gentle sing-song but Rhea was not looking at the handkerchiefs.

Philomena Francis was an unbelievably tiny spare woman, so dark that she was almost black; her hair was pinned into a knot with large black hairpins and she was decently dressed in blue gingham, with collars and cuffs worn thin; her hands and her face were worn too, with patience and toil, thought Rhea. Her fingers were pricked with sewing, her face lined. All her life seemed gathered up into her quiet and watchful eyes that were curiously serene; on a silver chain she wore a small model of some saint. She was, yes, humble and noble, thought Rhea triumphantly and, a few minutes later, she telephoned Valentine, 'Val, I have found your Nan.'

The meeting between Valentine and Philomena when Rhea took her to the office was, as she had known it would be, an entire success; Valentine was careful not to betray himself but Rhea could see, by the brightness of his eyes, how excited he was.

He sat, watching Philomena, talked to her and then leaned forward and said, 'Miss Francis . . . '

'Please to call me Philomena, Gentleman.'

'Philomena? It's a lovely name,' said Valentine. 'Well, Philomena, I should like to give you a test.'

In her ten years of film-making Rhea had seen the effect of those words on a great many people, a tightening of the face, trembling hope, determination, anxiety, apprehension, gratification. Philomena only clasped her hands in her lap a little more tightly and said, 'Yes, Gentleman.'

'Can you be here tomorrow at ten?'

Philomena was silent.

'Well?' demanded Mr Thunberger. 'Well? Why not?'

'I had to get a rickshaw to come here and it cost me twelve annas,' said Philomena.

'It cost how much?' spluttered Mr Thunberger.

'Twelve annas, Gentleman.'

'Ten cents! Cents! *Cents!*'

'Yes,' said Philomena sympathetically, 'and it will be twelve annas *back*. How can I come?'

A film test is an ordeal for the most experienced and Rhea had wondered how Philomena would take it. She seemed to accept it almost casually but she had not liked asking for leave from the Guild.

'José Pereira can take charge,' said the Superintendent who was far more excited than Philomena.

'*José Pereira!*' said Philomena scornfully. 'What does she know?' It was hard work to persuade Philomena to agree and she was silent as they drove in Mr Thunberger's car out to the studio for the test.

Valentine had given orders that Philomena was to be made up as little as possible and, as the shots were taken, he held her attention in the easy running talk that was his especial gift but still there was the hairdresser touching and retouching the black pins, the dresser smoothing out the collar, the make-up man dabbing his wet chamois to take off the sweat that ran down in the heat. Philomena, though, hardly seemed to notice any of them. The electricians turned and moved the lights, the cameraman ran his measure from Philomena's face to the camera. The sound boom came over, lowering the microphone above her head. Philomena remained quiet almost abstracted. Once she said to Valentine, 'Turn off that light, Gentleman. It's too bright on my face,' but most of the time she sat with a far-away look in her eyes. Is she quite all there? wondered Rhea and then she saw Philomena dart an acute look at the box she, Rhea, held in her hands, and it dawned on Rhea. 'She is not thinking about the test, she is thinking about the lunch box!'

Lunch boxes were sent from the hotel every day for all actors and crew; everyone grumbled roundly at them but, as Philomena had looked at hers, her face was transfigured; she looked at the sausage roll, the egg sandwiches, the cold salt beef, salad and paper napkin and slowly she had put out a finger and touched them one by one. 'Would they let me take it *home*?' she had whispered.

'But it's for you, to eat here,' said Rhea. 'We get one every day.' That was too much for Philomena to believe and, after she had eaten one egg sandwich, she closed the box. 'Ask the Gentleman if I can take it to show my sister,' she pleaded.

Rhea had seen the ground-floor room where Philomena and her sister lived. The sister was blind but earned money threading beads; through the beads and Philomena's handkerchiefs they said they had all they needed. Rhea had seen what they had: a bed, two wicker chairs and a table, some crockery and a picture of St Aloysius, the Saint of the Medal. Philomena and her sister were Children of Aloysius. 'And, Gentleman, you should be too,' Philomena said to Valentine. 'You look like him.' It was true; Valentine's dark eyes and his face, thin with feeling and fervour for this picture, were like the saint. 'Gentleman, won't you join with Aloysius?' she pleaded.

'But what did he do?' asked Valentine. 'I don't know much about him.'

Nor, it seemed, did Philomena and, a little at a loss, 'He was young when he died. He was good and wise. He thought what he did,' said Philomena.

'More than most people do,' said Valentine.

Philomena had worked in the Guild for twenty-seven years. 'All the week I work, sometimes from six in the morning till late at night,' and for this the Ladies paid her twenty-five rupees a week. 'About four dollars,' said Rhea, but Philomena was not resentful, she was proud and grateful. Now, as she looked round the great house, the garden palace of an Indian prince that the company was using as a studio, 'My Ladies have houses like this,' said Philomena with pride.

The test was excellent. 'Mr Morley, Valentine . . . ' began Rhea.

'The Gentleman?' asked Philomena.

'Yes, Mr Morley, Valentine, is very very pleased, and Mr Thunberger wants to sign you.'

'Sign me?' For the first time Philomena looked frightened.

'You will find him quite generous and kind.' Philomena looked more frightened still.

'We are going to do something big!' Mr Thunberger had said, 'And mind it gets plenty of space,' he said over his shoulder to Daffy, the public relations man. 'Here is this poor Anglo-Indian community; it goes to our hearts to see them. Don't let them think, because we're in films, we haven't got hearts, Daffy. Now listen. We're going to give that little old lady something that will set her up for life. For *life*, Daffy! Got that? She shall have five thousand rupees for this picture. Now isn't that big?'

'Not very,' said Valentine. 'You would have to pay Mooni twice that a week. It's under five hundred pounds,' but Mr Thunberger was right; it was big to Philomena.

'It's a fortune!' said the women at the Guild. They all came flocking round Philomena when they heard.

'Philomena Francis on the films! Philomena a film star!'

Even the Ladies on the Committee were interested.

'To be in a Valentine Morley picture! Why people would give their *eyes!*' said the Ladies.

'My God, what luck! What luck!' groaned the women.

'You might have prayed for it, m'n,' said the Superintendent but Philomena said nothing; only the black pins stuck out a little wildly from her hair, her face seemed more lined, her sing-song voice was a little uneven and her eyes were disturbed.

Mr Thunberger sent his car for Philomena to come, with the Superintendent as witness, to the Company offices for the signing of the contract.

'Now, Philomena,' said Mr Thunberger jovially, 'this is your lucky morning. Here we have your papers all ready for you!'

Philomena made no move; she sat facing Mr Thunberger, Valentine, Rhea, Daffy, Mr Thunberger's secretary and the Company lawyer but Rhea thought she looked curiously serene. Her hair was neat, the blue gingham clean and pressed, her face looked clear, her eyes bright. She did not speak.

'Come along. Come along,' said the Superintendent. 'My God, what are you waiting for?'

'I haven't made my answer yet, Gentlemen,' said Philomena.

'Your *answer?*' said Mr Thunberger. 'What answer?'

'My answer,' said Philomena.

'We will pay a rickshaw there and back for you every day.' Rhea was beginning to understand.

'A rickshaw! She will have a car.'

'And you get clothes and a room to rest in,' the Superintendent put in.

'And a lunch box every day,' said Rhea slyly and Philomena's lips opened a little.

'She will get five thousand rupees,' Mr Thunberger thundered to the room. 'Five thousand! Isn't that enough?'

Valentine quietly took Philomena's hand.

'You are so like St Aloysius,' Philomena told him tenderly but, as her eyes dwelt on him, Rhea knew she was inexorable, and, 'You see, Gentleman, you might call me to work on Tuesdays.'

'We might. Why not?' demanded Mr Thunberger.

'That's the day my Ladies fetch their handkerchiefs, I couldn't come on Tuesdays,' said Philomena.

'*Handkerchiefs!*' spluttered Mr Thunberger.

'Yes, handkerchiefs,' said Philomena.

'Philomena Francis, I have *told* you . . . ' began the Superintendent but Philomena went calmly on.

'And Fridays I give out the lace. It has to be cut *exactly*.'

The Superintendent opened her mouth but, 'It is valuable lace, I couldn't leave *that* to José Pereira,' and Philomena gently took her hand out of Valentine's. 'The salt beef was beautiful,' she said wistfully, 'and we should have liked the money but I am used to living very quietly. Gentleman, I might get tired,' she said to Valentine. 'I might get upset,' she looked at Mr Thunberger. 'I am sorry for you,' said Philomena, 'but I must say no.'

'If anyone could have talked her into it, it was you,' stormed Mr Thunberger at Valentine after Philomena had gone.

'I wouldn't talk her into it. I would rather use Mooni,' said Valentine.

'Mooni! Mooni!' Mr Thunberger's voice rose to a scream. 'At the last minute like this she will be able to stand us in for we don't know how much! She will ask a lakh of rupees.' He mopped his forehead and, 'You didn't want a professional.'

'Mooni is a film creature,' said Valentine. 'I can't do her any harm.'

'Harm!'

'Yes, harm. People let us pick them up into our world. You call it a celluloid world, don't you, Daffy, but it's real, quite real only it has a different taste; like goblin fruit, it spoils everything else. We pick them up into our world, keep them, pet them and drop them back into their own. Well, suppose they can't go back? People are not all as wise as Philomena.'

'Wise! It was the chance of a lifetime!' said Mr Thunberger.

'The chance of a lifetime, to spoil a whole life,' said Valentine.

'I don't understand.' Mr Thunberger was aggrieved. 'I don't understand.'

'No?' said Valentine lightly. 'But then – you are not a Child of Aloysius.'

The Oyster

'To travel is to broaden the mind.' Tooni, the sister-in-law of the young Indian student Gopal, had often told him that, but, thought Gopal, the mind can become so broad that it suddenly becomes a wild prairie in which no one could hope to find their way.

'When in Rome do as the Romans do.'

'To thine own self be true . . . '

Which?

Tooni loved axioms; she had taught Gopal these, she had 'instilled them,' murmured Gopal. Gopal earnestly intended to believe everything he was told, he knew that Tooni was sensible and wise but now, suddenly, in this restaurant in Paris his mind had become a howling wilderness. 'When in Rome . . . ' 'To thine own self . . . ' Which? He was not old enough to see that, by his travels and experiences, he was taking the only possible first steps to reconcile these conflicts by beginning to find out what he was himself.

Gopal was sweet naïve young, almost breathless with good will; yet he was dignified. René Desmoulins, the witty dark French senior-year student, reading English at the University, had seen the dignity and especially marked Gopal out, though he was twenty-three to Gopal's nineteen. Everyone was kind to the young Indian. Gopal was charming to look at; his body was tall, slim and balanced, his teeth and eyes were beautiful and his face was so quick and ingenuous that it showed every shade of feeling. They teased him about that but now he suddenly knew he was not as ingenuous as they, or he, had thought; he had come across something in himself that was stronger than his will or his desire to please. 'Aaugh!' shuddered Gopal.

Up to this evening, which should have been the most delightful of all, everything had been delightful. 'Delight-ful' was Gopal's new word. 'London is delightful,' he wrote home. 'The college is delightful, Professor William Morgan is delightful and so is Mrs Morgan and the little Morgans, but perhaps,' he added with pain, for he had to admit that the Morgan children were rough and spoiled, 'perhaps not *as* delightful if you see them for a very long time . . . The hostel is delightful . . . I find my work delightful.' He had planned to write home that Paris was delightful. 'We went to a famous restaurant in the rue Perpignan,' he had meant to write, 'it is called the Chez Perpignan. It is de—' Now tears made his dark eyes bright; he could not write that; it was not delightful at all.

Through his tears he seemed to see far beyond the white starched tablecloth marked 'Perpignan' in a red cotton laundry mark, beyond the plates and glasses, the exciting bottle of wine of which he had asked to inspect the label after the waiter had shown it to René. He saw beyond the single scarlet carnation in the vase on the table, beyond everything in the restaurant that had thrilled him as they came in; the dark brown walls with their famous old theatre posters – 'French printed in French!' Gopal had exclaimed as if he had not really believed that French could be printed – the serving table where a flame burned under a silver dish and a smell rose into the air, mingling with other strange and, to him, piquant smells, of hot china plates, starch, coffee, toast, old wine-spills, food, and clothes. He saw, beyond them all, the low tables spread for dinner at home, one of the dinners that he had always thought most ordinary, old-fashioned and dull, prepared by his mother and Tooni.

Gopal's family lived in Bengal; they were Brahmini Hindus and his mother kept the household to orthodox ways in spite of all he and his elder brother could do. Now Gopal saw her orthodox food, the flat brass platters of rice, the pile of *luchis*,* the vegetable fritters fried crisp, the great bowl of lentil purée, and the small accompanying bowls of relishes – shredded coconut or fried onion or spinach or chillies in tomato sauce or chutney, all to be put on the rice. He saw fruit piled on banana leaves, the bowl of fresh curd, the milk or orange juice in the silver drinking tumblers; no meat or fish, not even eggs, were eaten in that house. 'We shall not take life,' said his mother. Gopal looked down at his plate in the Perpignan and shuddered.

He had come to Europe with shining intentions, eager, anxious to do as the Romans did, as the English, the French, as Romans everywhere. 'There will be things you will not be able to stomach,' he had been warned; so far he had stomached everything. His elder brother, Jai, had been before him and had come back utterly accustomed to everything Western; when Jai and Tooni went out to dinner they had Western dishes; they ate meat, even beef, but not in their own home. 'Not while I live,' said his mother, and she had told Gopal, 'You are not the same as Jai. You are not as coarse.'

* *Luchis*: flaky, puffed, pale gold biscuits.

'Oh, I am, Mother,' Gopal had pleaded, 'I am just as coarse,' but now another shudder shook him.

'Are you cold, Gopal-ji?' asked René.

Gopal had taught René the endearment; he had thrilled to hear him use it, and even now he managed to smile, though in truth even his lips were cold. 'I am not at all cold,' lied Gopal. 'This is – delightful.'

If it had been the cold that upset him it would have been nothing; all Indians were supposed to feel the cold. Gopal did not mind the lack of sun, the grey rain, though several Western things were very strange to him; the perpetual wearing of shoes, for instance, made his feet ache, but he had liked his feet to ache; he had been proud of them when they ached, he felt they were growing wise. Now he wriggled his toes in his shoes under the table and would have given anything to be sitting with bare, sun-warmed feet. A feeling that he had not had all his time abroad welled up in him; he felt sick, sick for home.

He saw his own family front door, with the family shoes dropped down in a row at the entrance; he saw the hall, empty of everything but a rickety hat-rack that never had a hat hung on it – how could it? They wore no hats. He thought how he would come in, drop off his shoes on the step, and go to the tap to wash and take off his shirt, calling out to his mother and Tooni in a lordly way, 'Isn't there anything to eat in this house?' His mother, who never knew a joke when she heard one, would begin to shoo the maidservant and Tooni about and hurry them, and presently Tooni would bring him a few sweets in a saucer to keep him quiet.

> 'O Soul, be patient, thou shalt find
> a little matter mend all this,'

Tooni would say, and she would add, 'That is by Robert Bridges. Bridges was once Poet Laureate of England.' Tooni was always anxious to improve her little brother-in-law.

In Europe, Gopal had eaten everything. 'Roast lamb, kidneysontoast, baconandsausage,' murmured Gopal, and when René, who, being a Frenchman, had a proper feeling for food, had talked of the food they would eat in Paris, Gopal had not flinched, though some of it sounded rather startling to him – 'rather *bare*,' he had written to Tooni. 'Imagine sucking-pig, Tooni,' he had written, 'and René says it is laid out whole on the dish; *tête de veau*, and that is calf's head with its eyes and its brain all there. He says we shall have steak, *rare*, I don't know what that means but I shall find out, and oysters, I shall eat oysters. What are oysters? I shall find out. I shall come back more Parisian than Paris!'

René, the dazzling, elderly René, had asked Gopal home with him to Paris for the vacation. 'It is a delightful compliment,' Gopal wrote, 'and, let me tell you, there are not many he would ask, but he asked me!'

René, with his brilliance, his terse quick wit, his good looks, his ruthlessness and his foreignness, was venerated by the students and a little feared by the masters, which made him all the more popular and, when he was kind to Gopal, Gopal was completely dazzled. 'You are too good to me,' he gasped, and, shyly, 'You must love me very much.'

René had the grace not to laugh at him. 'You do not know *how* delightful he is!' wrote Gopal to his mother, and to Tooni he wrote, 'René is like Hamlet, only humorous; like Byron, only good.' He looked at these two comparisons and their qualifications; they did not seem to be enough, and he tried again. 'He is like Jesus Christ,' he wrote reverently, 'only very, very sophisticated.' For René, Gopal would have made one of those pilgrimages sometimes made by the devout in India, on which, at every step, the pilgrim measures his length in the dust.

On that thought, Gopal realised how much he missed the dust. What a funny thing to miss, he thought, but he missed the dust. He wriggled his toes uncomfortably in his shoes and thought he could even smell the dust of his own great Bengal town. It seemed to rise in his nostrils as he looked out of the restaurant window. Across the Paris twilight and its multitudinous lights, he seemed to see the small oil flares of the orange-sellers' booths on a certain narrow pavement near his home. He heard the car horns, not Paris horns but the continuous horns of the Sikh taxi-drivers; he heard bicycle-rickshaw bells, the shuffling feet and the pattering noise as a flock of goats was driven by. He wanted to go home, past the white oleander bushes by the gate, past the rows of shoes, up to his small room where, on moonlit nights, the shadow of the fig tree and the bars of his barred window were thrown together on the white-washed wall. How many nights had he lain on his bed and watched the shadow leaves move, stir gently in the heat, as he had wondered about going away far over the sea to travel in Europe, in England and, yes, in France? Now in France, he thought as he had never thought he could think, of that small room and the tears stung his eyes again.

René saw the tears and was concerned. Under the terseness and the sophistication René was simple and young and kind. 'What is it, Gopal-ji?' he asked.

'I – swallowed – something hot,' said Gopal.

'But you are used to hot things.'

'Yes, chillies,' said Gopal and laughed, but it was not

safe to think of such homely things as chillies; they made him see a string of them, scarlet, in the kitchen. He saw the kitchen, and his mother's housekeeping, which had often seemed to him old-fashioned and superstitious, now seemed as simple and pure as a prayer; as – as uncruel, he thought. His mother rose at five and woke the children so that they could make their morning ritual to the sun; many and many a time had she gently pulled him, Gopal, sleepy and warm and lazy, from his bed. She saw that the house was cleaned, then did the accounts and then, still early, sent Jai, as the eldest son, to market with the list of household things to buy and the careful allowance of money – few Indian women shopped in the market. When Jai came back, with a coolie boy carrying the basket on his head, the basket had a load of vegetables, pale green lettuce and lady's-fingers, perhaps, or glossy purple eggplants, beans, the pearly paleness of Indian corn still in its sheaf. There would be coconut too, *ghee*-butter and the inevitable pot of curd made fresh that day.

The kitchen was very clean; no one was allowed to go there in shoes or in street clothes, and before Gopal and Jai ate they washed and changed or took off their shirts. The women ate apart, even the go-ahead Tooni. All was modesty, cleanliness, quiet – and it does no hurt, thought Gopal, shuddering. All of it had an inner meaning so that it was not – not just of earth, he thought. Once a month was household day when the pots and pans and sweeping brushes were worshipped. First they were cleaned, the brass scoured with wood-ash until it shone pale gold, the silver made bright, the brushes and dusting-cloths washed, cupboards turned out, everything washed again in running water and dried in the sun; then prayers were said for the household tools, and marigold flowers and jessamine were put on the shelves. I used to think it was stupid, thought Gopal; I teased my mother and called her ignorant to believe in such things, but they made it all different, quite different!

'Gopal, what *is* the matter?' asked René and he laid his hand on Gopal's.

In India it is usual for young men who are friends to hold hands; for René to take Gopal's hand would have filled him with pride half an hour ago; now he flinched, and the intelligent René felt him flinch and took his own hand away and looked at Gopal closely. 'Explain what it is,' suggested René gently, but Gopal shook his head. He could not explain; how could he tell René that, for the first time, he saw not what the world did to Gopal but surprisingly what he, Gopal, did to the world?

Last night he had found out what 'rare' steak is; he had cut the red meat and eaten it, only thinking of the redness going into him and wondering if he could get it down, could 'stomach' it; now, suddenly, everything was in reverse. René had ordered the famous oysters and Gopal had looked so doubtfully at the plate of grey-brown shells and the strange glutinous greenish objects in each, that René had laughed. 'Pepper one, squeeze a little lemon on it, and let it slide down your throat,' said René. He had shown Gopal and Gopal had copied him but, when Gopal squeezed the lemon juice on his oyster, he had seen the oyster shrink.

'But – but it's alive!!!'

'Of course it's alive. It would be dangerous to eat it otherwise. If they served you a dead oyster,' René had said gravely, 'I should have to take it out and show it to a policeman.' Seeing Gopal's face, he said, 'Don't worry; it will die as soon as it touches you.'

'Auhaugh!' choked Gopal.

René had laughed. Now, remembering that, Gopal seethed with rage. His ears were burning, his cheeks and his heart; the plate with the oysters seemed to swim in front of him. Centuries of civilisation, of learning, of culture, to culminate in this!

'What *is* the matter?'

'You are a barbarian,' said Gopal in a low, burning voice. He trembled to speak like this to René, but he spoke. 'Your ancestors were running about in blue skins', said Gopal, 'when mine had religion, a way of life.' For a moment he stopped; René, in a blue skin, would look like Krishna; Krishna, the Hindu god, often had a blue skin, he played the flute and was the god of love and had many amiable peccadilloes, but Gopal hardened his heart against René, even in his most lovable aspects. It was this learning, this culture, this barbarism, that he had come all this way to share. I want to go home, thought Gopal. I want to go home.

'You all think we Indians should study your customs, why don't you study ours?' he cried to René. 'We could teach you a thing or two! Why should we have to Westernise? Why don't you Easternise? It would do you a lot of good, let me tell you that. You are cruel,' cried Gopal. 'You are not even honest. In England they teach children "Little lamb, who made thee?" and give them the roast lamb for lunch, lamb with mint sauce. Yes! You eat lamb and little pigs and birds. You are cruel. Cruel and barbarous and greedy and—' He broke off, trying to think of the word he wanted; it meant 'too much'. Ah, yes! a dozen dozen, thought Gopal, and hurled the word at René. 'You are *gross!*' he cried, and stopped. Though he was sitting down, even his legs were trembling. The effort had left him weak. 'You are gross,' he said in a whisper.

'You are perfectly right,' said René. He put another oyster down his throat, but there was something so mild, so tempered in his reply that Gopal was checked.

'These are things', said René when he had finished the oyster, 'that a man has to arrange for himself.'

It was not only a small rebuke, it was a suggestion made as Tooni would have made it, but of course Tooni was not as subtle and delicate as René, the same René who was now preparing to eat the last oyster on his plate – and he had a dozen, thought Gopal, when I had ordered only six! Subtle, delicate René, who was gross and delicate, fastidious and greedy, ruthless and mild. Gopal shook his head in despair.

'Travel broadens the mind.' Then if it is broad, thought Gopal, it has to include all sorts of things; he looked at René's hand, sprinkling pepper and squeezing the lemon – that clever, cruel hand. The world, when it was opened out, was not delightful; no, not delightful at all, thought Gopal. It had a bitter taste; he did not like it.

'When in Rome, do as the Romans do.' René was a Roman of Romans; now, with grace and elegance, he slid the oyster down his throat and smiled at Gopal. René agreed that he was not delightful; he was content not to be – no, not content, thought Gopal, looking at him; he knows that he cannot hope to be, all of him, delightful. And if René can't, thought Gopal in despair, who can? Excepting . . . well, it is easy if you stay in one place, in your mother's kitchen but if you go into Rome?

He thought of that steak, rare; he had eaten it and now in his mind there was a vision of the sacred bull that came every day to their house to be fed; he saw its soft, confident nose, its noble face and the eyes lustrous with thick, soft eyelashes; its cream dewlap swung like a fold of heavy velvet and it wore a cap worked in blue and white beads on its hump; Gopal had saved up to buy that cap with his own money.

'To thine own self . . . ' Tooni seemed very far away. Gopal turned away his head.

At that moment, René having beckoned, the waiter came and took the plate of oysters away.

'Now what shall we eat?' asked René and he asked, 'Have you ever tasted *vol-au-vent*?'

'How strange! It sounds like hitting balls at tennis,' said Gopal, beginning to revive.

'It isn't tennis, it's chicken,' said René. 'Would you like to try it?'

'Chicken?' The word seemed to hang in the balance; then Gopal asked, 'Is it new? Is it exciting?'

'Well . . . ' René could not say *vol-au-vent* was exciting. 'You may like it.'

'Nothing venture, nothing win,' said Gopal, and René gave the order to the waiter.

'This is delightful,' said Gopal.

KASHMIR

Kashmiri Winter
Poem

Big Sister, Hungry Sister, and the Greedy Dwarf of Ice,
these are forty days of winter, then twenty and then ten.
Can we fight them with straw sandals? And the leaping price
    of rice,
of charcoal and of salt and tea? Nothing is cheap but men.

The sisters have taken lovers, the blizzard and glacier,
the goose-white flakes of snow in the sky perpetually falling.
Why does Rashid lie so still, so still? His fingers flutter and stir.
It is the sisters calling; calling; calling.

The gravestones are narrow and small, lost in the snow, but free.
We shall be landowners then, Rashid, with no taxes to pay.
He has shut his big owl's eyes, now his rags are worth
    more than he.
Strip him and put him into the earth whom the sisters have
    taken away.
The iris* leaves cover the graves; their spears will
blossom between;
green is the Prophet's colour, but the snow has hidden
the green.

* In Kashmir irises are the symbol of money.

The Wild Duck

The wild duck came down on the river at dawn.
The river Jhelum in the Vale of Kashmir ran past
the villages below the mountains into Srinagar, that water
city with its seven bridges, its labyrinth of canals, and high
wooden houses with steps leading down to the water. Above
the town, houseboats and *doongas** were moored under the
chenar trees and the river ran by them softly, so held now
by the ice that the water was slow.

There is no vigour in the Kashmiri in the cold; he
hibernates. For five months in the year the land is sealed;
except for necessity no one works, no one washes, and most
people hardly wake. Even the boatmen close their boats
down with mats and huddle inside in their vast shawls.
Everyone – man, woman, and child – looks pregnant in
winter because, under their *pherans*, † a *kangri* ‡ is carried
against the stomach, is taken out with them, and even
slept with.

---

* *Doongas*: native living boats.
† *Pheran*: short magyar-shaped robe, men, women and children alike
wear of wool for the rich, padded cotton for the poor.
‡ *Kangri*: an earthenware pot filled with live coals and held in
a basket with a shielded handle.

In Subhan's boat, by day, the men in their shawls talked a little, and drank tea. At dark they went to bed and it was late into the day before they woke. There was nothing to wake them; Khaliq, the eldest son, heard his wife get up at dawn; she was an inconvenient woman and needed to go out, but he turned again with his face to the side of the boat and slept. It was at dawn that the wild duck came down.

Khaliq's wife scurried back to bed and the bank was silent. Even the domestic ducks, each tethered by one leg, slept with their heads turned and sunk in the feathers of their backs. There were hundreds of them along the river and it was fitting that the first light picked out duck colours, cream mottled with grey and brown and the bottle-green colours of drakes' necks. The grey was in the hulls of the boats, the browns in the mats that hung along their sides, while the snow was trodden to cream-brown slush on the banks. There was more grey in the trunks of the chenar trees and darker brown in their clusters of winter nuts; grey steps led to the water and there was grey in the sky with a promise of snow; even now, in the dawn, one occasional flake came down silently upon the water. The green was in the water, thick, translucent, turning lighter, more lucent as it lapped the steps; green, cold, dark with ice. The wild duck came down upon the green as silently as the snowflakes; she folded her wings along her back, rocking a little on the water as she settled.

She did not realise where she had come; anything she might have known was blotted from her by her hunger; she was starving. She immediately turned herself tail upwards in the water and her bill dabbled frantically in the weeds. She found what she wanted; the weeds were heavy with particles of ice but they were not frozen; there was life and food amongst them, and the wild duck went down and came up, came up and went down, and the point of her tail was turned to the sky that was slowly filling with the day.

She came up, dipped, came up. She had no feeling but of hunger; she was simply wild, come out of the winter sky, attracted by the weeds and at last she had found her food. The river here was warmer, its ice broken by the life of boats.

There were houseboats, *doonga* cook boats where the boatmen lived attached to the houseboats, wood-boats, rice-boats, grass-boats, ferry-boats, little boats; later in the day some would be poled along, handled under the bridges or paddled from side to side. All along the banks the litter of human beings lay silently in the coming light: dogs, bicycles, woodpiles, water-pots, tethered geese and fowls. Presently, from one boat and another, the first wood-smoke went up.

Close by, there was a village of tall houses with over-hanging balconies and a tall, thin screen of poplar trees; now, from the village, came the sound of clogs stamping on the ice, of a tap opened and water splashing on the ground. The wild duck came up and stayed motionless on the water with her head turned to the sound.

The village was upstream and upwind; the alarming sounds floated down but the current of the water still parted steadily around the duck, still steady, still undisturbed. The current reassured her; she paddled with her feet to keep her place; her feet were the colour of the orange peel that floated down in the debris of the river.

The sun had risen now and the watery winter light picked up fresh colours from the life on the river: orange peel, the colour of a child's *pheran* as she scooped up water in a *samowar*;* the light caught the copper colour of the urn and the jewel blue in the wild duck's wing; the blue distinguished her from the ducks by the boats, the tame, tied-up domestic ducks, fattening themselves with sleep and scraps and tidbits out of the weeds.

The weeds were a feast to the wild duck. To the west, where she came from, the lakes were frozen; the bare muddied shores, their reeds and wild iris blades were stiff in a shroud of ice. The hills at the foot of the mountains were brown and withered and the water in the rice fields was covered with a casing of ice. The only life and movement was from the far nets of the fishermen where the current stayed unfrozen in the lake, and from the fires of the charcoal burners on the foothills, with the rumble and fall of an avalanche up on the distant mountain. Then, in the boat, a mat was lifted and snow fell into the water with a loud splash. Startled, the wild duck flew out of sight. No one had noticed her yet.

Khaliq came into the front of the boat and sat down in his shawl. He felt heavy and dull. Khaliq was young lithe strong, the finest tallest man of a fine family, and a born boatman; his father was a boatman, his grandfather had been one, and his great-grandfather's father before him. They were hunters, too; when they were not in their boats they were camping in the mountains. They handled boats and guns. Both were as natural to them as their own hands.

Khaliq hated the winter, the inaction, the heavy dullness in his bones. He was overladen with the winter and, as he sat that morning, suddenly, like a crack in its ice, a memory came back to him. Last summer he had been out

* *Samowar*: Kashmiri tea-urn.

ibex shooting, convoying an English colonel into Yarkand beyond Leh and the valley of the Indus, very far away; up and up in strange, far gorges, empty except for the flocks that nibbled dusty herbage at the foot of the hills, the eagle's occasional cry, and the queer – even to Khaliq queer – broken notes of the flutes the shepherds played.

They had come to a village grown out of the gorge, where the houses were made of its colourless earth; there a glacier came down, and the village had a grove of quince and mulberry trees. Khaliq remembered how startling in that barrenness had been the colour of their green. The Colonel and he had left the tents, the servants and had gone up, up, up; two local hunters hauled the Colonel up the crags; Khaliq followed, carrying the guns; Khaliq, loaded with the rifles, had been the equal of the mountain men.

He remembered how, then, his body had been fulfilled; it was quick, awake, intense with power, its speed. Each movement of his body was as necessary as an animal's; the parts that were beautiful and the parts that were bad, the parts he enjoyed and parts that troubled him were all drawn up into a supreme wholeness; he was one, whole, for this purpose. Even his shoes were part of him, even the last hairs of his moustache were necessary to the completeness of this whole beautiful enduring Khaliq. They went up and up into a giddy rarer air, and then one of the local hunters pointed, and, following the line of his brown finger, they saw an ibex above them, standing on a pinnacle rock so high that it showed, through a cleft, a pocket of sky.

The hunter on the left of Khaliq said, 'Aaah,' in his throat; the sound dropped down the abyss like a stone; Khaliq had moved an angry hand but, as if the sound had truly gone down, not up, the ibex did not stir. There had been a quality of agony in that, a tension that hurt.

The Colonel was panting and Khaliq remembered how his own heart had hammered with thick thumping strokes that would have taken the breath of anyone less strong and whole than he.

The ibex was still there. As they watched, the sun glinted on its horns and it lifted its head to show the tuft and sweep of its beard.

They had to track silently to pinpoint it. Up again, again up and up, when not a stone must roll and fall. They were closer now, up and up, until through a split rock they saw a giddy slant of sky, crag – and the ibex. They had found a sight.

The ibex was below them now. They saw it with an eagle's eye; the planes of the peak were below them too, and the glacier that now had a blue reflection from the sky. They saw plane after plane of rock face, crags, and land slips and the thread of the river far below. The ibex was feeding, unsuspecting, eating tufts of herbage; to see it eat as the goat-kids had nibbled in the valley gave Khaliq a sudden pain that was the most complete moment of living he had known. That simple thing of the ibex nibbling had parted a membrane in his mind; always after that tame Khaliq and wild Khaliq were integral. He had said into the Colonel's ear, 'Now, Sahib. Keep low. A little to the left.' There had been no mistake; while the sound of the shot still rang from rock to rock, the ibex had thrown up its head, fallen on its knees and tumbled off the crag.

Why should Khaliq think of that now? All morning he kept thinking of it again. The memory kept coming up. He could not quiet it.

The morning in the boat went on as did all such mornings; his father's friends and his own friends came in to sit and talk; the air grew thicker between the matted sides of the boat, the hookah passed, and there was comfortable talk about money. Yet in Khaliq's mind he still saw the ibex, the climb and the crag against the sky. He saw the sun on the polished horns and the sudden blue of the glacier; he could believe in the feel of the horns as they lay in his hands after the ibex was dead, but had he really seen them flashing in the sun? The colour of the glacier seemed strange, faint and far; the village like one of the villages in his father's tales. Had he, Khaliq, been there only a few months ago, seen the green leaves of the mulberry trees, pitched his tent and bought wild honey from the people? He put away his fire-pot; it was too hot, and the folds of his shawl were heavy on his shoulders; he let it fall on the floor beside him as he sat but immediately he was cold and had to put it on. While they were talking, the wild duck came down again and settled on the water near the boat.

The tame ducks were loosened now; they were swimming up and down in tidy convoys, leaving a pointed wake. As soon as they saw the wild duck they came to her and swam around her. Immediately their shapes looked clumsy and dull; their quacking seemed platitudinous.

The wild duck rocked among them; except for the movement of the water she was utterly still and seemed to be floating on the water, not lying in it stoutly as they did. She paddled her feet, looking small light graceful, the colours of her markings clear in the winter daylight; the deep blue bar in her wings flashed in their eyes. Resentment spread in a ripple round her but she still paddled her feet and rocked lightly as the ripples grew.

In the boat the air grew closer, more odorous; the hookah passed to Khaliq and he inhaled with a melodious bubbling of its water, but it did not soothe him. The talk went on and he slumped with discontent, silent in his corner.

'Khaliq does not say a word,' said Mahomed, his friend.

Subhan looked at him. 'By his colour he is cold. He looks that he is sick.' He called through the partition, 'Bring Khaliq some good hot tea.'

Khaliq said not a word and presently Mahomed began to play on his two-stringed zither. It made a noise like a tortured violin; in the shrouded boat the noise was near and very loud. Khaliq's wife brought a bowl of salt tea from which a spiral of steam and a smell of spice went up. She pressed it into Khaliq's hand. The heat came through the sides of the bowl against his palm and irritated him; more heat, more soothing, more deadening down when he wanted not to be dead; his mind strained to be alive. The maddening little tune of Mahomed's bow went on around his ears. The noise, the heat and the closeness clashed suddenly in Khaliq's head; he gave a cry and threw his bowl of tea across the floor.

There was consternation, then a silence that was more unnerving than the music. Under his old folded turban, Subhan's face was outraged, it was incumbent on Khaliq to explain. 'Disgusting,' cried Khaliq. 'The tea is disgustingly cold.'

Relief and happiness. The tea was cold. What, to give the boy cold tea when he was sick and chilled! There was immediate shouting to the wives, scolding them, a jangling of earrings and whispers in the next compartment of the boat, and an immediate refilling of the *samowar* from the river.

A child was sent to dip. He had to put his head outside and, as he bent, he saw the conglomeration of ducks across the water; he watched with the *samowar* in his hand as a flake of snow fell directly upon the wild duck's back. The child saw the flash of brighter blue, the small neat shape, and his cry went up, 'Arman batukh. Wild duck. Wild duck!'

This time Khaliq did not betray himself. The cry went through him as if it were a spear thrust but he said nothing. He simply put his shawl down, stood up in one movement from his heels and was gone, swiftly but with no look of haste. He was no quicker than Mahomed, who had already loosed the *shikara*.* Khaliq stepped on to the prow. His father handed him a barbed spear and sent the light boat shooting out to the ducks in a thrust that was the real counterpart of the cry that had pierced Khaliq.

Now they were out on the river, Khaliq standing balanced on the prow and Mahomed sitting paddling in the stern. The boat was narrow and light and Mahomed's heart-shaped paddle broke water with hardly a sound; he kept the handle away from the side while Khaliq stood, poising the spear like a harpoon.

They sped towards the ducks, Khaliq balancing from foot to foot, tightening his muscles, tautening, loosening, alive and ready. The speed of the boat, the intentness of his eyes made a blur of the banks, the water, the sky; the sky was in the water, the water in the sky, there was again that giddy sense of height; planes spun below him, reflected planes; sky spun above him, but there was only one small object, small as the bead of a gun, in front of his eyes.

The wild duck had her attention on the tame ducks; they were a new experience for her and acted as decoys, swimming round and round her. She was watching them and her wariness, usually alert as the antenna of her tail, was lulled. She was bemused, unconscious of herself.

The spear hurtled into them. It came with a deadly

* *Shikara*: a small paddling boat.

95

aim, strong with speed, straight at the wild duck's breast. Her breast half rose in the water to meet it but a domestic white duck had risen before her with a quack that was to ring in Khaliq's ears for days and nights. His hand was empty, the spear had gone, and the white duck flapped and cried; the spear had passed through the end of its outstretched wing, deflected but not turned from its path, and one barb had struck the wild duck's breast, tearing the feathers. A morsel of flesh fell with them into the river where the spear furrowed a wave, was brought up and lay harmlessly floating in the water.

The boat was carried on by its impetus; it shot away to the farther bank, towards the mud and snow.

The wild duck struggled in the water. Blood oozed from her breast in a trickle that changed to a stream; it was dark on her breast, clear and scarlet in the river. She dipped sideways to the weeds while the white duck made loud rending noises, as loud as the shouts from the boats and the bank.

The exhilaration of the wind had died down from Khaliq's ears; the world had settled into its accustomed places as the boat struck the bank, driving into the snow.

'You have it,' cried Mahomed, looking back.

Mahomed was never accurate; he said what he hoped would become true but, at that moment, the wild duck gave a cry and rose into the air; she rose with a clumsy movement, splashing, scattering drops of water but her wings, even on the wounded side, could fly.

The white duck flapped but the wild duck lifted and flew; her cry floated down with the flakes of snow, a single mournful cry. The tame ducks paddled and eddied round the place where she had been as the stain of blood was washed out on the current; they dipped their bills looking for her, turning indifferent tails upon their wounded comrade.

Already from his boat the owner of the wounded duck was paddling out to parley with Khaliq; already Subhan, as Khaliq's father, was coming in a borrowed boat to defend his son and dispute the price. Mats were lifted up and down the river, waiting for the quarrel, while Khaliq's wife was quickly brewing the second tea with extra spices to soothe the episode away.

Mahomed turned the boat to go back for the spear and was silent. Khaliq knew it was for him to speak. Mahomed paddled, waiting.

'I thought I had it,' said Khaliq with a mighty effort as he knelt to get his spear. That was all that he could say. He could not laugh.

The Carpet

From the water in the silver bowl which the servant boy
held out to me came a scent of roses. As I washed my
hands – the Eastern custom before and after eating – our
Kashmiri host, the merchant Subhana who sat opposite us
at the low table in the room high above his Srinagar shop,
said, 'Do you know who first discovered attar of roses?'

'One festival night, Queen Nūr Jahān, to please her
husband the Mogul Emperor Jehāngir, ordered all the
marble water channels of the Grape Garden, the women's
garden in the Fort at Agra, to be filled with roses. In
the morning the hot sun shining on the decaying petals
brought to the surface a film of oil which, when skimmed
off, distilled the true fragrance of a rose.'

That might have happened, not in Agra, but in one
of the pleasure gardens that the Moguls built in Kashmir:
Shalimar, Nishat, Chashmishai, where the fountains still
play on festival days, the water runs in its channels from
terrace to terrace, and shades of Jehāngir and Nūr Jahān
haunt the marble pavilions. The Mogul Emperors, the great
Akbar, his son Jehāngir and grandson Shāh Jahān, who
built the Taj Mahal, were devoted to Kashmir. Every year
they left the searing heat of the plains and with their whole
courts made the long, arduous journey over the mountains
to the green coolness, the shining lakes and rivers of

the Vale of Kashmir, that paradise 'the Pearl of Hind'. They poured out riches and treasures on her, built their incomparable gardens on the shores of her lakes, planted mulberry orchards, poplars and groves of chenar trees; the great trees with their pale trunks and plane-like leaves we had picnicked under yesterday had been planted at Jehāngir's orders. Above all, they inspired her artists and craftsmen; the delicacy and beauty of her embroideries, the fineness of her shawls, the gold richness of the best of her papier-mâché work and carving owes much to the Moguls, especially to Jehāngir and his Persian queen.

We, too, had left the heat of the plains for the high coolness of Kashmir, flying, in a few hours, over the dust-hidden flatness of India, the foothills and the mountains that had taken the Emperors' cavalcades long weeks to cross. Arriving at the airport and the suburbs of Srinagar, we were disappointed; its modern buildings, petrol pumps, villas, neat trees, edged roads, might have been a town anywhere yet nothing, we soon discovered, could be more romantic and strange than the Old City, the Venice of the East. Tall carved wooden houses, on whose roofs tulips, iris, mustard grow, line the banks of the quick green Jhelum river with its seven bridges and busy water traffic. A network of waterways links the city to the Dāl Lake, and nothing could be more beautiful than this huge shallow reflecting spread of translucent water, backed by blue foothills, fringed with orchards, rice fields, flax fields, and groves of trees half-hiding villages of wooden houses. We hired a houseboat and, because we had come not only for a holiday but for rest and peace, moored it among the willows of an island, close to the shore but far from the fashionable inlet of Nagin Bagh with its rows of houseboats, its Club and bathing floats.

100

Most visitors to Srinagar live in one of these furnished houseboats which are attractive, built of wood inside and out, comfortable, even luxurious. Ours was not as grand as some but complete with electric light, a good cook and servants. When the spring weather grew warmer, we ate breakfast under a striped awning on the flat fore-part of the roof, which was edged with pots of geraniums and reached by a short ladder from the deck in the prow. The whole island was alive with birds: orioles, bulbuls, hoopoe, and the long-tailed paradise-flycatchers; kingfishers lived in the willows. From our high perch on the roof we could look far over the lake, in which were reflected hills, orchards and villages, a fisherman standing spear poised in a small drifting boat, to the snow-capped mountains that edged the vale.

Luckier than those tourists who usually come to Kashmir for only a few hurried days, we had several months in which to get to know her, to watch the changing colours as spring turned into summer. Kashmir is a land of flowers; each month had its own. We had come too late to see the first pink-flowering of the almond trees in the snow, but were in time for what Jehāngir called in his memoirs, 'the soul-enchanting spring' when the whole vale burst into a foam of cherry and then apple blossom; thick in the young grass under the trees were forget-me-nots, anemones, small wild pink-and-white striped tulips. Then, in one day, it seemed, the colours deepened and grew rich. Purple iris, to the Kashmiri the symbol of money, and lilac, the delicate Persian lilac, flowered along the lake shore and in every garden; big scarlet tulips grew on the house roofs. It grew warmer; roses were everywhere; in Shalimar they hung in sunset-coloured clouds over the old walls. Soon the huge pink cups of the lotus would cover the lake and then, although the lake is over five thousand feet above sea level, it would be too hot for a houseboat and we would spend our last weeks in tents among the pines and firs of the mountains.

From our houseboat roof we could see the traffic on the road that ran along the shore under the steep hills to the city, and watch the boats that passed all day on the lake: wood boats, grain boats, boats laden with water weed dragged up to be used as manure on the fields. The small light boats were *shikaras*, paddled with heart-shaped paddles, fishermen's *shikaras* and taxi-*shikaras* with embroidered curtains and cushions and labelled with ridiculous names such as 'Whoopee', 'Here I Come!', to attract tourists; some were driven by outboard motors that cut across the silence of the lake. Every morning, merchant *shikaras* would stream from the city towards us. Flower-sellers, their boats laden to the gunwales with bunches of flowers, came first and were difficult to resist. Confectioners had cakes in red boxes, and there were jewellers, traders in carvings and papier-mâché work bowls and lamps.

'Most of these are trash,' Subhana told us. 'Made for tourists, not for you.'

We first saw Subhana sitting under the awning of one of these *shikaras*, his hands folded under the grey *pashmina* of his shawl, his boat held by his paddlers at a dignified distance until the rabble should disperse. 'He is a rogue,' our friends were to tell us, 'and very expensive.' Subhana dealt in precious stones, embroideries, carpets, and was, as we were to discover, certainly expensive, but what we bought from him was the finest of its kind. As other merchants had done, he gave us his card; it was the fashion, it seemed, to give themselves names like Suffering Moses, Patient Job, Subhana the Less, Subhana the Worst – Subhana is a very usual name in Kashmir. Our Subhana, whose humour was never deprecating, called himself Subhana the Best.

That first morning, he did not sell us anything but, seated on our deck, showed us some Kashmir sapphires and told us stories, amused us. Kashmiris are a handsome even beautiful people and Subhana, immaculate in his soft grey *pheran*, shawl and white turban, looked as rich and handsome as the things he sold. His skin was a rosy glowing brown, his beard perfectly kept, his eyes large and dark; he always wore a huge agate ring. The next day, the day of the Spring Festival, we met him in Nishat. He, too, had come to see the fountains play and was strolling along the crowded terraces, holding a spray of lilac in his hand; a servant boy carried a box behind him. Later, from a distance, we saw him sitting under a tree unpacking the box. Surrounded by an interested crowd he was unfolding layer after layer of soft rice paper, laying out jewels that winked in the sunlight on a square of red cloth. Holiday or no, it was business as usual.

Subhana came often to see us, and we went to his shop on the lower floors of one of the tall houses below the Third Bridge. The shop was a cavern, a jewel-case of beautiful things. We had not really wanted a shawl, but we soon possessed one, a shawl so fine and soft that it really might have been drawn through a ring; it was embroidered with the five symbols of Kashmir, the bulbul, lotus, vine, iris, chenar leaf, and the kingfisher, emblems found so often in her embroidery and carvings. We bought a papier-mâché lamp worked with a design of birds flitting through a tracery of flowers, although we did not care for papier-mâché work. 'You have seen only the cheap bazaar boxes and bowls, painted with chemical colours,' said Subhana, 'this is of our traditional craft, made of fine paper pulped and moulded by hand. The blue is lapis-lazuli, the red carnelian, the gold real gold. Of course it is expensive. You, Lady Sahib, need the best.'

Although we did not know it, we were being led by stages through those lazy days towards the particular carpet that Subhana, long ago, had decided we should buy. When he first unrolled it on the deck of our houseboat, we tried not to show our delight. It was not large, about seven feet by four, and of a silky fineness but heavy when we turned it over to see the closeness of the knots and the pattern showing clearly on the reverse side.

Subhana smiled at this display of knowledge. 'Feel the quality of the pile,' he said, 'thick and smooth, like the fur of a cat in cold weather. It is an old, old carpet, woven perhaps in a village in the hills of Persia.'

To us, its formal flower patterns glowed with the true Kashmir colours: deep and pale blue, rose and apricot and crimson, touches of green and a warm cream. When we heard the price, 'Take it away at once,' we said and Subhana laughed.

That was the beginning of a campaign that lasted several weeks. We saw the carpet again in his shop, where its colours seemed to have grown deeper, richer. 'I will *lend* it to you,' Sabhana said, 'so that you can feast your eyes on it.' For two days it adorned the sitting-room of the houseboat. He might have added, 'Once it has been in your possession you will find that you can't live without it.'

We let him take it away again. Subhana lowered the price slightly, and our offer rose, but the gap was still too wide. Then, on the day the first lotus bloomed and he learned we were soon leaving for our mountain camp, Subhana asked us to lunch with him in a room high above his shop – a Persian luncheon, a feast.

The room, with its panelled walls and windows looking out over the city, was small; it held only a low table, a long cushion-like seat for us and one for Subhana; the ceiling reflected the light from the river below. Serving boys came and went, bringing course after course – a Persian feast traditionally has thirty-six courses but this, mercifully, had been reduced to eighteen. Subhana ate nothing; he sat watching us benignly, and drank cinnamon-spiced tea. Spoons and forks were provided for us; the art of eating correctly and gracefully with the fingers was one that he must have doubted we knew. This was a Moslem household so no alcohol, only sherbet, was served with the meal, but it is possible to become slightly drunk, certainly stupefied, with food. We ate and ate, knowing that it would be bad manners, even insulting, to refuse anything. There were mutton balls stuffed with spices, apricots stuffed with lamb, pilaff, fish in coconut, saffron rice, honey rice; each course was delicious, perfectly cooked, but soon Subhana's face seemed to gaze at us through a golden mist, the room to contract and expand.

At last it was over; the bowl of rose-scented water, the folded towel, were offered again. 'Now you must have some spiced tea,' Subhana said, 'or would you prefer coffee? And I shall show you some carpets – perhaps something more to suit your purse.'

As we leaned back, replete and a little breathless, against the cushioned wall behind us, boys unrolled carpet after carpet, laying them one upon the other beside us. There were crimson and white Bokharas, pale and formal Kirmans, Kishan, Tabriz, Turkoman, carpets from Agra and from Kashmir's own factories. The room glowed with colour as Subhana told us each carpet's name and history; they were beautiful but our eyes knew what they wanted to see. Subhana knew too. As the coffee tray was set on the table between us, he made a sign – and there was our carpet, spread over the rest.

To us, a cheque book and fountain-pen looked out of place in that small rich room; Subhana regarded them with satisfaction, as well he might. 'You won't regret it,' he told us. 'Wherever you go, however far from Kashmir, while you possess that carpet you will have a feast for the eyes, a feast for the soul. And now, let us seal our bargain in coffee, Turkish coffee that only we of the East can make.'

When my cup was empty, I held it up to look more carefully. It was made of the thinnest, finest jade set in silver.

'Perfect, is it not, Lady Sahib?' came Subhana's oil-and-honey voice. 'Six cups, the finest workmanship. I would not part with them to anyone else but, to you, they are for sale.'

Red Doe

They were riding down from the upper pastures to get Ibrahim married.

Every spring in the Himalayas of northern India, the Gujars, shepherds, and the Bakriwars, literally 'goat people', drive their flocks up from the plains to summer in the high valley and plateau pastures in the mountains where they have left their huts.

Now Ibrahim felt pleased and important. There was only one person whom he knew or felt anything about and that was Ibrahim, himself, the son of Ali, the Chief Elder of the Clan; naturally the morning was pleasant and important to him.

It was so early, as they rode, that the grass in the valley far below showed in sheets of pale dew in the sun; the ice streams shone, pale too, bright with the early reflection of the sky. Later in the day it, and they, would be a deep August blue and the grass would unroll, mile after mile, with the belts of coloured flowers that came in the spring and summer; here spring was June, July; summer lasted two months, October brought the first snow, and the rest of the year was winter; these were the high mountains of the northwest Himalayas that led into Ladakh or Little Tibet.

When the cavalcade of young men reined in to rest

their ponies whose legs shook from the steep way down, Ibrahim could feel and smell snow in the wind; it blew from the peaks that towered all round them on the sky-line. Snow sometimes came in summer, 'But not today,' said Jassoof, Ibrahim's friend, laughing. 'You don't want frostbite today, ehu, Ibrahim?' The mountains ringed the valley, eagles flying in endless circles below the crags. It is windy there, thought Ibrahim, watching them. He could hear the waterfalls that looked, from far away, like the crystals he often found in the streams and sold on the way back to the plains.

Ibrahim's people, the goatherd nomads, moved in clans, each with its Elders. Ibrahim's Clan had its encampment on an alp thousands of feet above the valley, in the last spruces of the forest where a small meadow spread its gentians, primulas, anemones and geums in the grass. Ibrahim did not notice flowers – to him they were part of the grass, grazing for his father's goats – as he did not see the colours of the glaciers, the wicked blue of their crevasses, the mountains or snow slopes of the passes; he only knew how many marches away each was, which led to fresh grazing grounds, which snow bridges would hold. If he saw the eagles it was only to judge the wind; deer were for hunting with spears, bears were to be avoided, the little wild marmots who sat up on their tails to scream at humans were for him and his friends to throw stones at. Ibrahim knew goats and ponies; he did not count them as animals but as part of his life; he lived with them as he lived with his father, mother, uncles, cousins, friends, especially Jassoof, but they were themselves, he was Ibrahim; he was not responsible for them. He had had nothing to bother him until now when the time had come for him to have a wife.

'We want a good strong one,' his father had said. He had said that too of the Yarkandi pony they had bought last year. 'Not too young a girl, not less than fifteen, and strong.'

Ibrahim had nodded and felt a sudden curious tingling that seemed to come in his palms, his thighs and the backs of his knees, and his throat was suddenly parched. 'I want her to be beautiful,' he said.

'Beautiful!' cried his father shrilly. 'A beautiful woman is nothing but a nuisance. No, she must be strong, not too young, and of good stock.'

'And beautiful,' said Ibrahim and his father leaned forward and slapped him on both cheeks. Ibrahim was a young cock among the youths of the Clan, but his father still slapped him when he thought it would do him good.

After that Ibrahim looked at every woman he saw, wondering if she were beautiful. They all looked beautiful in the distance but that was the way they walked, straight from heels to head, keeping themselves to themselves. Now Ibrahim's eyes came prying among them and he saw things he had not seen before: how their bare feet and ankles looked small under the folds of their black and red pleated trousers; how their black tunics swung out below their breasts, the full hems sewn and weighted with a load of white pearl buttons; how their veils hung loose but showed, under each, a flash of blue from the bracelet-size cap they wore on their heads; and how their silver jewellery sounded as they passed in and out of the huts and the tents, round the fires and through the flocks. Their anklets chinked, and their necklaces and earrings; Ibrahim began to hear that chinking in his dreams.

When the Clan was on the march, the men drove the flocks, rode the ponies, and carried nothing unless it were a favourite child or a newborn kid. The women walked, carrying the gear of the camp on their heads, netted bundles of heavy iron cooking pots and platters; they carried their babies in slings, or a child on a hip; they dragged the dogs on strings and drove the slowly moving sick hurt animals. They were also often in childbirth; the caravan was always having to stop and wait for an hour or two, or even longer, while a woman gave birth. Then the Elders were pleased; they liked to see the caps and hoods of the children running about in the Clan, but the young men were impatient, though they often had to do the same thing with the herds. This new Ibrahim looked and wondered; some of the women seemed to him beautiful, none of them beautiful enough.

Now the day had come and he and his cavalcade rode down through the forests which grew more and more balmy as they came lower in the valley. Here there was a noise of wild bees and of larks above the meadows where the larch and spruce trees opened on small alps of grass heavy with clover. The air smelled of resin and of honey. Ibrahim, on his grey pony, sniffed it and, sniffing, he found, suddenly, that he could smell himself.

He had been given a new turban of bright blue muslin, and he wore the wedding blanket, dark blue with fringes, a scarlet border but his homespun coat was his own because he had no other coat. He smelled of wool and wood-smoke and sweat and goat; to smell himself made him feel more than ever full of Ibrahim and more and more he felt that tingling excitement.

The chief moment of his life, up to now, had been when his father had bought him a saddle but it was not a new saddle and had been used by his uncles and cousins as well as by his father and himself. It was the same when he was given his first full-size blanket, the homespun, hand-woven blanket-shawl that all the men carried like a plaid on their shoulders; the blanket was not Ibrahim's, it was family property.

Now the tall young Jassoof led a small pony with an empty pad. Ibrahim, and no one else, would lead it back and his wife, for the first and probably last time in her life, would ride beside him, back up the mountain to her new home. She would be his own; no one would have the right to own her or use her except Ibrahim.

They were riding faster now that the path had grown more gradual as it neared the valley. They rode like Cossacks on their small thick-set ponies, which were prized if they were short below the knee, well shouldered, with thick necks and thick manes. The mares had their foals trotting loose after them. Manes and blanket-ends flew in the wind as the cavalcade crossed the wooden bridge above the noise of the river, bursting in thunder out of the mountain; the hooves of the ponies made an equal noise on the wood. Spray blew in their faces exciting them; Jassoof let out a cry that made the others whoop like demons or wildcats to answer him. The ponies plunged and broke into a gallop that swept them into the valley with the ground drumming under the galloping hooves. Then, at the far head of the valley, where a glacier spread and melted in streams across the grass, they saw a single dark speck, a hut.

Thick loud whoops came from every young man round Ibrahim, jokes cracked across him, and they all began to whip their ponies. The grey kicked out though he had not been touched, and broke away from the rest into a glade where mares and foals, running wild, were grazing on clover and forget-me-not. Ibrahim knew he had seen the glade before; something else he had seen but he could not remember what; then it came into his mind that it had been when he was riding, that it had been exciting too but a different excitement. They had been hunting. Hunting? Then he remembered. It was a doe, a red doe, which had run, startled, out of the spruce trees, in front of them into this glade.

He remembered the shout that had gone up from the men; it seemed to him the same as was in his ears now. The whips had been lifted then too and the ponies were lashed as they spread galloping in a circle to head off the doe, while the older men, who had the spears, held them ready. Ibrahim had come up with the doe as she turned, driven back; he had come so close that he could see her red sides heaving for breath, her ears pressed down, her muzzle strained as she ran. Ibrahim had swung his pony on to her and she turned again but sideways as the old man, his father, had thrown his spear and she fell, pinned through the neck to the ground. It was Ibrahim who jumped from his saddle to cut her throat before she died.*

There was something else he could remember that he did not wish to, and he reined in his pony and rode slowly through the glade. He had to remember himself bending down with the knife in his hand and the doe, with blood gushing from her neck, had looked at him and he was suddenly alone with her. No father, no Jassoof, no others were with him then; it was only Ibrahim and the doe, and he, her eyes knew, had done this to her. Suddenly, it was he who had been stricken because he was no longer Ibrahim, himself, he was Ibrahim and the doe.

* Mahomedans can eat meat only if the throat of the animal is cut while it is alive.

'Allah! Kill it!' shouted his father. 'Owl! It will be dead before you cut!' Dazed, Ibrahim had taken his knife and killed her.

When she was dead she was dabbled with blood to her scut; her small pale tongue hung out with blood welling still from her mouth; her eyes slowly glazed, hiding their meaning, but all day he could not forget. Perhaps he had never forgotten, but now, as his pony began to trot out of the glade, went into a canter, then to a gallop as it joined the others, he chuckled; he had remembered he had refused to eat the venison that night and that seemed to him, now, exceedingly amusing.

They came to the hut. It stood by itself on a fertile grazing plain fed by a hundred ice-springs. There were silver birch trees and flowers; buffaloes and goats were grazing. Other huts and tents stood on the edge of the forest and smoke rose from cooking fires. Children stopped to watch these stranger men on their little horses as they splashed through the stream then rode in a circle round the hut, faster and faster with cat-calls and whoops, as the Elders and the men of this Clan came out to meet them.

The feast began. Inside the hut the fires were smoking; the men sat in a circle, dipping their hands into the iron bowls and platters of pilaff, roast kid, chapattis and apricots stuffed with mutton, curd and honey rice. Ibrahim, feeling young, oddly light and thin in the place of honour between the Elders, was grateful that he had to be silent as became a young man. He was shy but he was also very hungry. The food was good and he ate until he felt his stomach expanding and his legs growing warm with well-being, which travelled up his back into his neck and face so that he began to smile feeling jovial again and suitably old.

All the young men knew where the women were.

There was a cloth stretched tightly across the hut, nailed from wall to wall, that kept bulging and swelling as bodies pressed against it and from behind it came a continual sound, whispering, giggling and laughing, and that soft chinking of jewellery. Ibrahim looked and felt more warm and jovial than ever. The tea bowls came round and the hookah, with its gentle liquid bubbling sound, passed from hand to hand. Ibrahim thought that, through the cloth, he had caught a gleam of scarlet – wedding clothes with a dark veil, new cap and new jewellery that chinked, chinked, as Ibrahim had heard it in his dreams. She was young – he knew that because they had been born in the same year, the year of the great snow. She was sworn to be strong, but Ibrahim was thinking now of a woman's skin and knew that he had often felt it without noticing; he marvelled as he remembered how it was fine soft, much softer and finer than his own; he thought of a woman's hair and knew he had seen it loosed, another woman hunting in it for vermin, combing it, long, blue-black in the sun. He thought of a woman's body, of his body and hers, hers soft where he was hard, hard where he was soft so that they matched, and he began to tingle so that he had to dig his nails into the backs of his knees as he sat.

Ibrahim thought they would sit there for ever. He took his turn at the pipe politely, he drank bowl after bowl of tea, he listened politely to the jokes, barbarous jokes that made the cloth shake; he smiled until he thought his cheeks would crack, and still it went on and on.

At last Jassoof stood up. Now the time for politeness was over and the raw thing would be done. Now the Elders would lead out the girl and put her on the pony with the empty pad; Ibrahim would take its hair rope in his hand and ride away with her.

Silence had fallen on the hut. The men separated into two dignified groups; the Chief Elder, with his sorrel-dyed beard in the centre of his Clan, Ibrahim in the centre of the other. Presents passed and the bride's dowry, a bundle of clothes, two good iron pots, and a few coins, was given to Jassoof; Jassoof's young brother stayed behind to drive up five chosen goats. Now the men went outside and the Elder went behind the cloth. Presently he came back and with him, supported on two sides by women, came Ibrahim's bride. All Ibrahim could see was a shape bundled in a red blanket, the top of a bowed head. The blanket was wound to her nose and she kept her head obstinately down so that the edge of the blanket met her veil.

Ibrahim longed for her to look up until, looking round, he saw the same longing on the faces of all the men standing round. Some had wives at home, some were not yet married but, as they stared at the red bundle, they had the same look, hot with lust, longing and Ibrahim suddenly felt angry and resentful. Had she looked up then, he would have beaten her when they reached home.

She did not look up. With soft slow small steps, quite unlike an ordinary woman's stride, she went to the pony with the Elder, who lifted her on to the pad and put the rope into Ibrahim's hand. The women began to call out and laugh, a few to weep; the Elder stepped back and stood, tall and courteous, while the girl's father looked with expressionless eyes away to the mountains and Ibrahim's friends began to bit up their ponies and tighten their girths.

Jassoof held Ibrahim's grey pony. Ibrahim stood with the rope in his hand while his bride sat on the pad, motionless, her head down. He began to run his hand up and down the pony's neck, a cross impatient hand; he ran it up to the pad, down the neck to the head, up to the pad, and then he noticed that every time his hand moved nearer the pad, the girl shrank back. It amused him and he moved his hand more, brought it nearer her each time, nearer and nearer, so that first it touched her blanket, then the soft folds of her trousers and then, unexpectedly, warm and firm, her thigh. The round warmth and firmness of it astonished Ibrahim so much that at first he left his hand there through sheer surprise, an equally astonishing sweetness filled him, added to his longing, and then he felt her tremble. He felt her tremble and, at that, triumphant strength filled him and he pressed his hand hard against her until something warm and wet fell on the back of his hand.

It was a tear.

Ibrahim stood still. The drop lay on the back of his hand; as he looked at it, it seemed that the Elder, the father and Jassoof and the young men and the women disappeared. Ibrahim was alone with this girl, sitting helpless on the pony, and he had made her cry. The trembling fear passed from her into him. He did not want to be married, he did not want to take her away into his home, his hut and his bed, all the days of his life. He dropped the hair rope and turned away as the pony veered round.

The Elder caught the pony and courteously returned the rope to Ibrahim, showing no surprise. Jassoof caught his shoulder. 'Owl! Can't you hold your own wife?'

'I don't want a wife,' said Ibrahim.

'You will tonight,' said Jassoof.

Ibrahim mounted his pony and Jassoof pulled up the small pony beside him so that its nose touched Ibrahim's leg. A throng pressed round them and the calls and shouts sounded across the valley. Someone laid a whiplash across the ponies' tails; they started forward, jerking through the streams so that the riders were splashed to their knees. Ibrahim saw the girl draw up her heels; her hands came out of the blanket to clutch the pad. They began to gallop over the grass, feeling themselves more men since morning, pleasantly fillipped and excited. The married ones began to think of their wives, the young ones eyed Ibrahim's and wondered when their turn would come; gradually the feeling spread to Ibrahim. The girl stayed hidden but under the blanket she was there as warm, round and firm as the promise of her thigh. Presently he, Ibrahim, would undo that blanket.

He knew that, but he knew too that he could not be only Ibrahim again; and, as they rode back into the red doe's glade, he knew that what had started in him with the doe was in him with the girl's tear and would be in him now for ever.

All the same he began to laugh as he led the way home.

The Little Black Ram

'Your mother was a prostitute, the daughter of a prostitute!' The children called that after him and the Elders and the women cried, '*Shaitan!* Seed of evil!' Ali did not care; his father was dead, he had no mother, and his tongue was so quick that he could give them worse abuse than they gave him.

The Clan prized courage, spirit and hardihood as they prized endurance and strength but they were gentle and had the shepherd spirit; the boy, Ali, born one of them, was as different as if he were differently coloured, a firebrand with no sense of reason; he was a young thief, a bully, noisy, quarrelsome, and turbulent, against everyone with everyone against him. 'What shall we do with him?' sighed the Elders.

Only Ezekiel, the oldest of them all, thought something could be done. 'He will learn,' said Ezekiel.

'But when, when?' asked the exasperated Elders.

'Presently,' said Ezekiel. That did not solve the question of the fights among the boys when Ali was sent to help with the grazing, nor of the upsets among the ponies when he was told to drive with the men, nor of the milk stolen from the buffaloes, the calves panic-stricken from his chasing when he was sent to keep the herd, the food stolen and the girls teased when he was left at home. Ali had no kinship with anything or anyone unless it were the Clan's self-contained, self-reliant goats with their wicked yellow eyes and strong horns. '*Bhai*,' one of the boys might by accident call him in the warmth of play or work and he always retorted, 'I am not your brother. I have no brothers.'

Only, once, when he was lying on a rock, drumming his heels in the sun, putting back his head to feel the air on his face, shaking his black curls back from his short, broad forehead to look up at the vault of sky and dare the sun with his eyes, did he hear a sound that made him become suddenly still; it was a pipe that Mahmud had brought up from the plains and kept in his waist knot and played to himself, a thin bamboo pipe. As Mahmud played it, Ali could not bear it; it gave him a feeling of piercing sadness and emptiness so that he did not know what to do with himself. It made him too much alone, a speck on the mountains, a nothing, a grain among a million million grains; he wanted to go and look into the face of another boy, to go near him if it were only to kick him, or to clasp one of the great goats round the neck even if it turned its horns on him. Mahmud played on and the feeling swelled in Ali until he felt he would crack in pieces with it; he jumped down off the rock on to Mahmud and began to beat him.

'My pipe! My pipe!' Mahmud screamed but the pipe was crushed against the rock as they rolled over. Mahmud's turban came off, Ali lay on Mahmud and pummelled him, an elbow on his chest, his hand holding Mahmud's hair while the other fist drove unfairly into his soft sides and belly. That made Ali feel himself again and his eyes looked as wicked as the goats'; when the other boys dragged him off, Mahmud was half-stunned and bleeding. 'You rascal! You good-for-nothing! You young cock!' said Abdul Kharim,

120

the Chief Elder, when Ali was sent for. Abdul Kharim slapped him on both cheeks and sent him a five days' march with old Ezekiel, who, besides being the oldest, was the crossest man of the Clan, to buy sheep and drive them back.

'Sheep?' said Ali in disgust.

'Sheep!' said Ezekiel. Ali thought that sheep did not please Ezekiel either.

The nomads seldom keep sheep; they breed small horses and buffaloes and goats, suited to movement and to enduring the steep and difficult mountain climbs to summer pasturing; sheep are too slow, too soft for this, but occasionally, just before the clans move down, the Elders will buy a few sheep to fatten and sell in the plains for the Indian autumn festivals. These were small fat-tailed sheep, prime for mutton and for wool; Ezekiel and Ali drove them back and, before the first day was over, Ali hated their soft woolly helpless bundled bodies and their bleating voices. 'Take care, young owl!' said Ezekiel, giving him a box on the ear. 'Would you have that ewe in the river?' Though his ear was tingling, Ali shrugged and scowled, then laughed scornfully; he would have liked to put the whole flock in the river. Ezekiel gave him another blow to teach him manners.

Late that night the same bleating ewe was delivered of twin lambs; one of the lambs was black. 'Here, *shaitan*, here's a brother for you at last,' said Ezekiel, lifting it.

The black lamb, still with its cord hanging, red and wet, its legs dangling, lay in Ezekiel's hand. It had barely drawn breath but struggled fiercely to get away and tried to kick with its tiny hoofs that were cloven and black. Its forehead, where the black curled hair was still sticky and damp from the birth, was, indeed, very like Ali's but on its head it had the mark of embryo horns; it was a ram. 'Take it

121

and keep it warm,' said Ezekiel, 'while I see to the mother. Warm the other one too.'

Ali picked up the white-grey lamb without interest but, when he put the black lamb under his coat, felt it move against him and butt him with its head, he was filled with a feeling that was the opposite of what he had experienced from Mahmud's pipe; he felt stirred, not to emptiness but, as he warmed the lamb, to fulfilment. When he felt its warmth he felt the warmth of himself, Ali. He looked down at the small curled black head nuzzling on the rags of his coat and he was puzzled to find that this feeling was good.

After that he and the ram were inseparable. It was not, Ali said, that he liked the ram but that it liked him; he pushed it away and even threw twigs and pebbles at it but it followed him everywhere he went. It would not stay with the sheep but went after him among the goats and was not in the least afraid of them. It could balance on its small hooves as well as any of them; its legs grew as strong as springs, and its body grew hard. 'Allah! It will be tough eating,' said Ezekiel.

The boys teased Ali, which made him angry. When the Clan moved back to the plains, they taunted him with the butcher. 'Butcher. Butcher will take your ram.' Ali half-wanted the ram to go; the boys threw stones at it and that made another unaccustomed feeling rise up in him, though the throwing of stones was customary enough. The thought of the ram stoned, or slaughtered by the butcher, made his stomach feel queer. He wished Abdul Kharim would give his order quickly but in the end the Elder did not send the rams to be killed and, when the spring came and the flocks were driven back to the Himalayas, the ram was with them, trotting at Ali's heels. When it felt the mountain grass under its hooves and smelled the snow wind scented with honey from the flowers, it went wild with joy. It jumped with all four feet off the ground as it went cavorting and shying over the glades, shaking its neck and small fat tail with ecstasy. Ali suddenly laughed aloud, and in the same glee lay down and rolled in the flowers himself.

The ram grew large and strong; the hard small curves of its horns showed; and now, for the first time, Ali felt how troublesome and tiring another could be. On the strong mountain air and grass, the ram grew wicked; it would run at the women carrying their water-pots from the streams, and raced among the children, sending them flying; the women clamoured for it to be killed or sent away. Abdul Kharim looked and heard and frowned, the boys threw more stones at it; everyone was against it and still it went bounding, kicking, and butting round in the camp among the flocks, a small black tornado. 'Take that black devil away from the folds.' 'Aie! It has broken into the hut and eaten the fresh curd.' Then it ran at Rahman's Bibi when she was fully pregnant and she fell and had a premature birth; the baby lived but the anger broke out more fiercely. 'Slit its throat. It should be killed. Ill-begotten. Seed of evil. Shaitan!' The feeling rose in Ali again, mingled anger and strangeness; the strangeness was that he felt that he was no longer Ali alone but Ali and the ram; again it was like the feeling from Mahmud's piping. He felt for it what he had not felt for himself, and he caught the ram by its neck and dragged it away from the camp to the goats. That night he did not go into the huts but slept out of doors with the goats and the ram.

Two days after that it ran at an unbroken colt, which swerved in fright, throwing its rider Daveed, a big sullen boy; even the women laughed while Daveed scowled, picked up a stone, and hurled it in temper at the ram. The stone, too large to throw at an animal, broke the ram's leg.

When any animal in the herd broke a leg, they sent for Ezekiel. If it were a clean break he, with his old clever hands, would delicately set it, splint it, and hold the splint in position with a criss-cross network of light twigs tightly bound up the flank so that the whole limb was held stiffly when the animal moved; it was skilled work and took a long time. Now Ezekiel came and looked at the black ram. Ali felt himself tremble. No one liked the ram, they all wished it dead; would Ezekiel cut its throat? 'It's a clean break,' said Ali and his tongue came out and licked his lips. Why could he not say a simple thing like that without having his tongue become dry and his heart beat?

Ezekiel grunted.

'It would not be – difficult?' asked Ali. The ram lay with its sides heaving in pain, moisture running from its nose. There was silence, till Ezekiel grunted again and, squatting down on his ankles, took twine out of the deep pocket of his homespun coat and began to work. He sent a boy for twigs and told Ali to hold the ram. 'You are my father and mother,' said Ali humbly.

The ram kicked hard with the other leg as Ezekiel pulled its broken leg straight. '*Inshallah!*' cried Ezekiel and swore at Ali for not holding it better. The boy pleaded under his breath with the ram to lie still, for he was afraid Ezekiel might grow cross and leave it but now he saw what patience the old man had; it is animal nature to kick and struggle against pain and the ram struggled wildly. Ezekiel went steadily on till the leg was straight in the splints and the network, woven with twigs, tied with twine, was so firm that even the most energetic ram could not kick it off.

A reverence for Ezekiel began in Ali, who had never felt a reverence for anything or anybody before; Ezekiel was taciturn and cross but had this power of healing which he would use for a bad boy and a plaguey young ram. When at last the ram was released it scrabbled with its feet on the ground and quivered, blew through its nostrils, and stood upright. 'In three weeks it will mend,' said Ezekiel.

'God is great!' said Ali with unaccustomed politeness; his eyes glowed. At that moment he thought Ezekiel greater than God.

It was four days later that Abdul Kharim ordered that the Clan should move, crossing the high passes that led down to the valley of the Liddar on the other side of the great range. 'It is too late in the season,' grumbled Ezekiel. 'It is mad! The last pass is one of the worst in the mountains. If we get snow, there will be death. His father would not have done it.'

They left the huts standing under the trees and began their march through the gorges and up the mountains to the passes. Day after day they journeyed on, passing rivers of water and rivers of ice, great glaciers perpetually frozen; climbing crags and precipices, wandering across high unknown glades, making a new camp each night, stopping sometimes for an hour or two for the birth of a child or of a late calf.

Ali, as he had the lame ram, was given the task of driving all the sick animals; usually only a woman or the mildest of the boys had patience to do this but now the fierce Ali left camp first in the morning and came in late, long after the others, sometimes long after dark. He had an old she-goat, once the leader of her flock, huge old tufted ugly and maddeningly obstinate; with her was a spotted half-grown goat as disobedient as she, and a small fat kid he had to carry. They all had broken legs, splinted like the ram's, and they walked, limping and hopping, stopping and whimpering, trying to lie down or break away. Only the black ram limped faithfully behind Ali which made Ali go on and not rebel, though it seemed to him that each day was a moon of days; he lashed the old she-goat unmercifully but brought them all safely into camp each night. 'That is a changed boy,' said Abdul Kharim.

'I told you he would learn,' said Ezekiel, smoothing his beard. Then he added, 'But he will have to learn to do without the ram.'

'But it is with the ram that he is good.'

'He will learn to do without the ram,' said Ezekiel. 'One day he will have to learn.'

They camped one evening not far from the foot of the last pass; its crags loomed over them and the night was cold, without stars. 'Snow,' said Ezekiel, sniffing the air. 'I told them! Snow!'

Next day they were early on the march and Ali was soon left behind. That morning the old she-goat seemed possessed of the devil and the young goat followed her; it was not till long after midday that Ali drove them, dragging the kid in his arms, up among the rocks at the foot of the long cleft that led up to the pass.

He stood and looked at it, putting his head far back. It towered for perhaps two hundred feet over his head, sheer rock in which the wind, ice and water had hollowed a curious funnel up which it was possible to climb on a spiral stair of great toothed rocks. Eleven young men, with shouts and cries, were shouldering a buffalo up it; the buffalo panicked and lowed, but up it went, while the rocks gave the echoes back. The whole air round was filled with lowing, bleating and cries; there was pandemonium at the foot of the cleft; women were weeping; men sweated and swore, dragging and beating the animals. The boys were carrying up the kids on their necks; the goats went neatly their own way but the buffaloes had to be pushed and lifted, the ponies swung by necks and tails from rock to rock. Slowly the crowd thinned and, from far up and out of sight, bleating and whistles dropped through the air and faded out of hearing.

As the afternoon went on, the light changed and flakes of snow began to fall; the flakes grew heavier and the work became feverish. Women, young men and boys went up and down, up and down. Ali left his sick ones grazing and worked, carrying kids, pots and bundles until his legs and back ached. One by one the other boys left and went on with the flocks, but Ali had always to return to his hurt animals. He knew they must be the last.

When most had gone he took up the kid and gave it to another boy to carry while he came back for the half-grown spotted goat; but the step from rock to rock was too high for him to manage with its weight and if he dumped it on each rock ahead of him, it came down too hard on its injured leg. The men swore at him to keep out of the way and, crestfallen, he brought the goat back and waited. At last only he, two goats, the ram and a pair of small white ponies were left. The snow was now falling so fast that Ali wondered what it would be like up on the head of the pass. 'If it is a blizzard – aie!' He rubbed his hands inside his knees and chafed his bare ankles, trying to keep warm, waiting for someone to come back. The animals quietly cropped the grass with the snow falling on them.

At last he heard men coming. There were four of them with the young Daveed. Ali sprang to his feet to help them. 'It's big snow,' they called to him as they started with the ponies, two men to each. 'Hurry! Everyone has gone,' they called. 'We shan't get over if we are not quick. Quick. Hurry.' Daveed swung the young spotted goat up on his shoulders. 'Hurry. Come along, fool! What are you standing there for? Hurry. Be quick.'

'But – these,' cried Ali for the old she-goat and the ram.

'We won't wait for those. They are no good. She is old and he is *shaitan*.'

'But – ' cried Ali running towards them, 'they can't come alone.' The ram, as it always did, came after him to see, butting him aside with its head.

'Leave them,' called the men. 'All that can't run are to be left. Hurry! Hurry!'

Ali's cry followed them. 'I have brought them so far . . . '

'Turn them loose. Hurry.'

'Come down again. Come back for us,' called Ali.

One of the men turned round. 'Little fool. You must save your own skin. Come on.'

'Brother . . . '

Daveed's voice called back, mocking, 'I have no brother.'

Ali cried, 'For the love of God . . . '

Nobody answered him.

Soon, far above, the voices died away. The quiet was eerie where the noise had been. The snow fell and the light dimmed to twilight. The old she-goat went back to her greedy cropping but the ram stayed by Ali; it was cold and wanted his warmth, its breath steamed over his hand. *'Inshallah!'* muttered Ali, bending to pick up the ram.

Its weight for him was tremendous, far more than the weight of the young goat. He staggered with it to the first rock and across to the second, but his arms were torn almost from their sockets while his heart felt as if it would burst his chest. On the third rock he had

128

to dump the ram and he felt the jar as its leg met the rock and heard its sudden surprised hurt bleat. '*Nahin!*' said Ali and, setting his teeth, struggled up with it once more and managed to get it safely to the next rock, but the sides of the funnel and the snow were whirling dizzily round him and he had to sit down and put his head on his knees. 'And there are fifty rocks to get up, fifty, seventy, a hundred.' Ali could not count but he remembered the rocks leading up. The snow was coming thicker, blown in gusts and eddies whirling in his face, choking him, and it was not twilight now but getting dark. He could hear the old she-goat bleating; she knew that she was left. He sank his head down on his knees again.

'Aaa-li!'

'Yé. Yé,' called Ali, springing up. 'Yé. Come down! Come down! There is one more. Come down.'

'Come up,' called the voice. 'Hurry. Little fool. Come up. You will be lost,' called the voice. 'You will break your neck.'

'Come dow-n,' called Ali.

'Come up. Come up. Come up.' He could hear the voice going away. 'Co-me u-p, Aaa-li . . . '

All that he could see of the ram was a bulky blackness by his side, but he could feel it warm and close. He bent and with another effort picked it up again. Holding it against him for a moment, he looked up, then turned back; struggling, slipping, dashing his feet against the stones, bruising his elbows and knees, he got back to the foot of the cleft; there, sobbing for breath, he lay down, curled with the ram in his arms, letting the snow beat down on them, but the animal did not understand and indignantly broke away, struggled and got up, bleating.

It was senseless to lie there alone. He stood up, a

great fear sweeping over him. Numbed with cold, he shook his legs and shoulders while the snow blew in his eyes and mouth. He looked up at the cleft again. There, somewhere ahead, if he could catch up with them, were his people, warmth and food. The she-goat had come back and stood by the ram, looking at him, waiting. Slowly, Ali unwound his short turban from his head and slowly wound it on again, winding the cloth over his head and ears, round his neck and over his mouth. The she-goat and the ram still stood waiting. Ali gulped and turned towards the cleft.

The old goat remained where she was but the ram at once hopped and scrambled after him. He heard it bleating as it tried to get up on to the first rock; its hooves scrabbled as it fell back. It bleated. Ali went on up the cleft. The bleating followed him a little way; then he could hear it no more.

Alone, he went up the cleft as easily and quickly as any strong young goat; the snow gusts hit him without hurting him but he had another pain; almost breaking him was that same piercing emptiness and sadness that had come from Mahmud's pipe. There was nothing to break now but himself; the ram was gone.

As he found the top of the pass, he came out on a level cliff of rock and began to run towards the track that led down through the gathering darkness. The feeling grew until he felt he must break, and then there was a strange relief as he felt something on his face, drops of something warm and wet that appeared to come out of himself, out of that aching pain; strange drops for, when they were on his cheeks, they froze to ice though when they came out of his eyes they were fresh and warm. As he ran towards the path they came faster, till they prevented him from running. He stood still while his tears fell fast.

CALCUTTA

Miss Passano

Miss Annie Passano stood in the station yard with her
boxes and bundles, the birdcages and the monkey, and
turned her money over in her black leather bag. I had
better take a rickshaw, she thought, but it will have to
be two rickshaws with all this luggage, what an expense.

She was a big fat middle-aged Eurasian woman with a
dark flat face. She wore a white cotton dress that was too
tight in front, flat black strapped shoes and a big white
topee that sat uneasily over her heavy bun of hair that
was as black and coarse as a horse's tail. She felt sick,
giddy and ached all over. Her head pained and it was full
of the rumble and thump of the train – no wonder, tossing
about in that stuffy compartment while the Hindu widow
chewed nuts all through the night. What a journey it had
been, and all for nothing.

She looked angrily across the yard to the river. The
glare hurt her eyes. Although it was only six o'clock the
sun was already up in the bright empty sky that was as
colourless as an old dishcloth.

If I take a carriage it will come cheaper, she thought,
looking at the rows of ponies drooping between their
shafts. They had chains of blue beads round their necks
and shining brass on their harness but Miss Passano knew
that there were sores under their collars and that their ribs

were like birdcages. 'Poor creatures,' she said. 'No, I'll take two rickshaws.' She raised her umbrella and the rickshaw men swarmed round her.

When the rickshaws moved out of the yard the monkey sat on her lap holding on to her dress with frightened fingers. At her feet the blue and white birds were silent with terror at the bottom of their cages. She said, 'Don't be frightened, we will soon be home and then you shall have water and seed, and for this little one there will be milk and a plantain.' Although it was so hot she pulled her plaid rug over the monkey's head to shut out the noise.

It was very hot sitting in the rickshaw as the stream of traffic crawled slowly towards the bridge. Miss Passano felt as if pieces of hot gravel had got under her skin, and her thighs were already stuck together with sweat. She thought the same weary thoughts over and over again.

I did right, she thought, I saw the old man once more. The fare was heavy but I did right to go. They should have been glad that I came all the way from Calcutta. Such a trouble it had been; no one to leave to look after the house and to feed the birds, no one but that silly child, Lily – dear God only knows what she has been up to all alone in the house. And, after all, no one was glad to see me. Old vulture, that is what Fred called me, and that stuck-up sister-in-law of mine was most unpleasant. I had to leave two days after the funeral – my own father's house too. As for the will – I might have known it – nothing, nothing for me. The old man died unforgiving, no religion in his heart in spite of the priest standing there. Not a rupee, not an anna, not even a picture or a piece of china – and me a lonely woman with an orphan niece to support, a great useless mouth. Nothing for me but the birds and the monkey; no one had wanted them! They said, 'Take the old man's monkey, Annie, or we will have it put away. Take the birds too and then you can keep the good brass cage. Come, Auntie, a few more for your menagerie,' and I had not the heart to leave the poor creatures with that mean ungrateful lot – yes, mean, ungrateful, cruel, same as most everyone else. Well, I have never had much use for people. I would rather have my dogs and birds any day.

Miss Passano took her handkerchief from her bag to wipe her wet face and trembling mouth, and stared defiantly round her.

The rickshaws were wedged in the slowly moving lines of traffic. Buses rocked and clanged down the slope from the bridge; lorries, cars and carts crawled slowly up it. The buses had rattling white tin sides with red letters on them. The wooden wheels of the bullock carts squeaked as they turned. Everywhere people swarmed and dodged, their heads bobbed through the traffic like the heads of swimmers caught in a dangerous current. A thin mist hung over everything, and overhead the low brassy sky sent the heat and the rising din beating down again as if it were a wide brass gong.

The beggars came round the rickshaw holding out their hands and showing off their sores. Miss Passano did not notice them until a half-naked beggar woman, with a goitre hanging from her neck like a hideous third breast, put her hand on the rickshaw and started her singing whine. Then she shouted, 'Be off with you!' and hit the hand with her umbrella. 'Too many people,' she muttered crossly, 'too many people everywhere.' Poking the rickshaw coolie in his straining wet back she called, 'Move on, lazy, are we to dawdle here all day?'

Beside the rickshaw was a bullock cart from the

country. It was full of fruit and vegetables and on top of the load that was already too heavy sat or slept a whole family. The bullock's head was near Miss Passano's knee. She saw the red wound under the wooden yoke where the flies were thick. She could see into the big oval eye that was full of gentleness and patient suffering. She sat up straight and opened her mouth to curse the driver in the words she had so often used before to other drivers. 'I see your number, O evil one. I'll report you to the Society, and now I go to fetch a policeman. You know the law, so many maunds and no more!' but she did not say them. Not today, she thought, sinking back and looking away, I won't look today. Each poor bullock in this crowd is like this one, but today I won't see them, I am too upset in my feelings as it is. Then she said to herself, 'When I get to my place I shall have a cup of tea, and then I shall undress and Lily shall stand and pour cold water over me. I shall feel better then.'

The rickshaw moved on. There was a dead dog lying in the road; it would lie there, she knew, until it was ground to nothing under the wheels; it was certain that no one would take it away. She could not help thinking of the thousands of homeless starving dogs that skulk round the streets of the city, no one caring what death they come to die. Then she had to think of the thin resigned little ponies; of the unhappy lives led by the buffaloes; of the countless struggling bullocks and the silent birds in their too-small cages. 'Dear God, what a world!' she moaned. 'Shall I never get back to my place?'

The air was full of dust and the smell of petrol. Sweat ran down Miss Passano's back until she thought she must be sitting in a pool. She fanned her face with her bag.

There was a smell of blood on the air. She looked

round and her heart jumped as she saw a cart that had moved up beside the rickshaw. It was full of meat from the slaughterhouse and flies made a dark cloud over it. She was sick and faint as she looked at the hacked and half-skinned nightmare of red and white but she could not look away. She sat and stared at the dirty cloth that did not hide the poor load under it.

Miss Passano wanted to get down from the rickshaw and run away. She wanted to curse and shriek, but she sat still, trembling a little, her lips set in a hard shocked line, holding a handkerchief to her nose. I should like to die now, at once, she thought, I cannot bear any more.

Suddenly she prayed aloud although she did not know it, 'Dear God, please do something. If I were you I should wave my hand and say, "Let there be no more men." ' As she prayed, she saw a paradise of green fields covered with flowers and divided by streams that ran as clear as glass. The blue skies were thick with silver stars and the gold sun sent down only gentle rays. On the cool grass lay the creatures, healed of their wounds, at peace for ever. It was quiet; there were no voices, no sound but the bleating of the lambs and the singing of the birds. Only she, Annie Passano, was there, tending them and caring for them for ever and ever.

Tears came into her eyes. She sat in a dream, hearing only the beating of great wings, blue and white, of angels or of birds. She did not know that the rickshaws had left the bridge and were now running through quieter streets, and she did not move when they stopped outside her gate. The coolie spoke to her; with a start she came to herself. She was only a fat bewildered woman climbing heavily out of a rickshaw.

She fumbled clumsily in her bag and paid the rickshaw

men, dropping the few pieces of money into their hands as if she hated to give them anything at all. Taking no notice of their angry protests she opened her gate. She called, 'Lily! Lily! Come here!' in a querulous voice.

Lily came down the stairs. She was a thin, dark girl in a dirty dress; her black hair was screwed up in tight plaits and fastened on top of her head. Her shoes were too big for her; they made a loud clopping noise on the wooden steps. She smiled timidly at her aunt, holding one shoulder higher than the other.

'Child, you should have been at the gate to meet me,' said Miss Passano. 'Come now, where's your voice? The trouble I've had to teach you your manners and still you don't know enough to open your mouth and say, "Good morning, Auntie." '

'Good morning, Auntie,' said Lily in a voice as thin as a piece of cotton. She kept her round black eyes fixed anxiously on her aunt's face.

'Come, child, don't stand there gaping at me. Tell the boy to take up the luggage,' said Miss Passano. 'Here, you can carry up the birdcages – be careful of them now, and you can take my rug over your shoulder.' Miss Passano went slowly up the stairs holding on to the banisters.

The birdcages were too heavy for Lily, they bumped on the steps as she struggled up the stairs. She panted as she answered Miss Passano's questions. 'Yes, Auntie, all the canaries are well. Yes, Auntie. I fed them every day. All the dogs too. They are well. No, Auntie. I never went out. Yes, Auntie—' Her shoes caught on the fringe of the rug; her thin damp fingers slipped from the shiny brass rings. The cages fell to the bottom of the stairs, turning over and over as they went. There was a loud squawking from the birds inside and a few blue and white feathers

138

drifted out and lay on the steps. The dogs started to bark and Miss Passano's canaries set up a shrill screeching from their cages on the verandah.

Miss Passano put the monkey down on the landing and turned on the child. 'You wicked careless girl,' she said thickly. 'You cruel child! I'll teach you to be cruel to helpless creatures.'

Beating down the thin uplifted arms she smacked and hit until her own arm was tired. Then dropping the crying girl on the floor she staggered to her basket chair on the verandah. She was breathing heavily and her big breasts were shaking. She sat with her knees apart, her head back on her old red cushion.

Slowly the mists of anger cleared from her brain. She heard the tinkling of china as the boy put the tray on the table beside her, and from somewhere behind her came the sound of gentle sobbing; it was soft and monotonous, it soothed and quietened her nerves. She felt better.

Presently she bent down and undid her shoes and kicked them off across the verandah. Then, taking a deep breath, she unhooked her stays, and leaned back again, folding her hands on her stomach, sighing with pleasure. A soft breeze came through the chiks* and dried her wet forehead. Her mind was now a pleasant blank.

The sun climbed higher and, finding holes in the chiks, made white patterns on the floor. From the streets came the sound of distant traffic and the nearer cawing of crows but it was quiet on the verandah. The boy had rescued the birdcages, setting them on an old table on the verandah; the birds cooed gently together, the monkey had had

* Chiks: rush blinds which are let down over windows and on verandahs. Water is sprayed on them to keep the house cool.

139

his plantain and milk and was asleep on the plaid rug beside her; only Lily's sobbing, unnoticeable as rain, went on and on, hopelessly on and on as if it would never stop.

Miss Passano did not hear it. She was asleep.

Mercy, Pity,
Peace and Love

At the top of his foolscap paper Ganesh had written
'Mercy, Pity, Peace and Love' carefully underlining it
in red. The words looked highly ornamental and he was
pleased. 'Are they not the best words?' asked Ganesh.

It was towards the end of the long hot colourless
Indian day. The light in the market was growing richer
and perceptibly softer, though the sun only shone as a lit
spot behind the clouds that pressed down on the city. The
light filled the market square and the stinking lanes that led
around it, where taxi horns and rickshaw bells sounded and
mud from the rain puddles splashed the fronts of the open
booths. In spite of the rain it was no cooler; the freshening
expected October weather had not come and, for all the
softening enriching light, the scene was squalid; there was
a smell of rotting garbage and cess, flower scents and
incense, a strong smell that helped to weight the dullness
of the air.

Calcutta's Newmarket is a huge one-storeyed building,
spreading over half a mile, with aisles of concrete between
its shops. The shops range from the silk and plate-glass-
windowed jewellery shops to the humble curd-seller, with
his measuring cup and pot of fresh curd on his hour-glass
shaped wicker stand. Everything for everybody was sold
under the Newmarket roof.

In a shop on the market front young Ganesh Dey was finishing his thesis for his doctorate. The Puja holidays were near and he knew, if he did not finish now, it would not be finished. His father had dragged him out shopping to buy Puja presents but persistently, in any quiet moment, on any shop counter, Ganesh wrote a few lines, just managing to curb his bad temper when continually interrupted by his father.

October is the month of the great festival of the goddess Durga, when young men and women all over Bengal return to spend the holiday at their homes and now a tide of sentiment was creeping over the market and over the shops. They were crowded with Hindus buying everything that their households needed for the festival days: coconuts, ghee,* sugar, fruit, sweetmeats and cakes; Ganges water and rice flour for making ritual patterns on the house floors; garlands and flowers; jewellery, new saris, shirts, shawls, children's clothes, caps, shoes and toys.

Ganesh's father, old Gurudas Dey, was buying, by weight, a pair of silver earrings for his daughter-in-law, Ganesh's wife. The earrings were charming, silver filigree worked into a miniature pair of pagodas with a fringe of silver bells, but Ganesh did not look up from his writing.

'Ganesh, you should pay attention to me.'

'One moment, Father, please.'

'Sushil is more help than you,' said his father bitterly. Sushil, a little boy, his youngest son, was so excited that he ran backwards and forwards to the car, looking at the parcels, looking into the other shops, talking, calling, laughing and asking torrents of questions without waiting for a reply.

* Ghee: clarified butter.

Old Gurudas was left to choose the earrings by himself; he picked them up one by one from the tiny weighing scale and looked at them through his spectacles. 'Do you think she will like these?' he asked for the twentieth time. 'She mustn't complain at home.'

'M'mmm?' said Ganesh.

'The saris are so expensive this year. But if you think . . . '

'M'mmm,' said Ganesh.

'And what is the subject of this thesis that takes up the whole of your sense?' asked Gurudas, drawing his tired old legs up on to the seat of his chair so that he sat more comfortably cross-legged. 'What is it about?'

'The nature of human love,' said Ganesh.

'What do you know about love?' said old Gurudas. 'Human nature is a very curious thing, I can tell you. Then so, I suppose, is love. I never really thought about it, but I do think you ought to help me choose these earrings for your wife,' but Ganesh was not listening.

'There is no merit in loving those near and dear to us,' he wrote in his beautiful copper-plate writing: 'Mercy, pity, peace and love . . . ' (Blake): 'their quality is not strained . . . ' (Shakespeare): 'the greatest of them is love' (St Paul). None of them seemed quite apposite but he did not know quite why.

A small car threaded its way into the market square and turned to park beside the Deys' ornamental Buick. The small car had no chauffeur or boy attendant but was driven by a young Englishman with his wife beside him; sitting between them on the seat was a grave well-behaved little spaniel with well-burnished copper-coloured ears. The young man's face was drawn and pale as he bent to take the key out of the ignition and then beckoned to a boy to come and watch the car.

'Hugh, you look so tired.'

'I had a hell of a day in the office.'

'You need, how you need, to go home!'

'Home, England,' he laughed. 'Next year perhaps but . . . ' He glanced at her. 'You ought to go now, Sue.'

'Not without you.'

'Think of heather, and Cornish butter, and draught ale, and fishing the De Lank on the moor.'

'They can wait. I shan't go without you.'

'And rabbits for Nibs. What about that, Nibs? Think, he has never seen a rabbit,' and, as he opened the door of the car, he put his hand tenderly under the dog's long silken ear. 'No, he has never seen a rabbit, little Nibs.'

Not far from the car rank, close to the jewellers' range, was a heap of garbage thrown out in the square. There had been no sun that day to disinfect it and its stench was worse than usual. Round it, as always, there prowled sick starving creatures, peasants driven by hunger in from the villages or poor derelict families from the city streets.

There was a skeleton-thin woman of no recognisable age among the shadows gathered round the heap, but she was not looking for scraps – purplish rags of chicken skin, old ant-ridden bones, soft putrid vegetable stalks and leaves; she stood asking, endlessly asking, someone to look at the baby in her arms. '*Ma. Bapu*,'* she whined at the men and women, '*Ma* . . . ' She wore a grey-white sari wound round her hips and across her breasts which were dry and useless as a crone's; the baby wore nothing at all and, as it lay back

* *Bapu*: father.

over her arm, its ribs and the little pit of its stomach looked up at the sky. It was quite motionless; only its head lolled as she moved, now and again it showed the whites of its eyes. 'Look at my baby,' the woman moaned. '*Ma. Bapu. Bhai.** Look at my baby,' but no one had time to look; they were all too busy looking in the garbage pile.

The Catholic church of Our Lady of Sorrows stood in the lane at the side of the Market, its steps kept clear of beggars and lepers by the uniformed porter. Its doors, so fictitiously wide open, showed a dark cool interior lit by candle flames that dipped in the wind made by expensive electric fans. Several people had dropped in for the Angelus that was ringing, measured and slow, from the tower; there was a nun; a man in a white duck suit; a group of poor Anglo-Indians; three American soldiers; two women.

'Ding,' said the bell, 'Ding-dong-dong . . .

' . . . The Lord is with Thee
Blessed art Thou among women
And blessed is the fruit of Thy womb, Jesus.

'Ding-dong-dong-dong . . . '

Ganesh wrote: ' "Mercy, pity, peace and love," says the Western Poet, whose method, without wonder or the dawn of understanding is to mention with sledgehammer direction (i.e. not subtly) the qualities that he would wish to imbue in the public mind. How childish and how crude.' He read it aloud to see how it sounded and, 'Isn't that rather rude?' asked gentle Gurudas.

Mrs Melanie de Souza, Chérie and José, paused on the steps of the fruit market opposite Our Lady of Sorrows.

* *Bhai*: a term meaning brother, but also applied to friends or cousins.

'Shall we not go in?' asked Mrs de Souza. 'Just for a moment, not?'

Small thin-elbowed José looked longingly across at the church but of course she did not say anything. She knew Mrs de Souza was not speaking to her; her aunt, unless she were angry, spoke to herself or to her own little girl, Chérie, who to José was anything but dear, a spoilt consequential little girl, perpetually whining, 'Mummee. Mummee.'

'Just for a moment,' said Mrs de Souza. She wiped the sweat from her face with a scented handkerchief, scent so strong it gave José nausea; the powder on Mrs de Souza's face failed to hide its swarthiness, the dark skin that troubled her so much, as did her black hair, though it was magnificent, in contrast to the small black eyes José dreaded; they were so quick they seemed to snap. Chérie, miraculously, was fair, with red curls which made her more cherished, but José was even darker which shamed her aunt again. 'You take after your father, not *my* husband's family, I'm glad to say, m'n,' but now, 'Just for a moment,' said Mrs de Souza. 'Chérie, we ought to go in. It will not take a moment.'

A moment, a quiet moment. José could have begged for it but still she did not speak.

'Mummee, we have to buy Dr Domel's wreath.'

'Yes, yes, of course, darling. But it is the Angelus and we are so near.'

José looked startled. She had heard the bell but her ears had not had the sense to take in what it meant; it had simply made her long to sit down on the cool wood of a pew. If she could have eased the ache in her back and legs, just for a moment! But perhaps it was a selfish thought, it had prevented her from thinking of the prayer, and so it was quite right that Chérie should whine,

'No, Mummee, we won't have time,' and that they should turn away towards the flower range.

The thoughts of Mahomed Iqbal, the Mahomedan livestock seller, had also turned to prayer; the sun was going down, it was time for him to unroll his prayer mat and he had not yet finished his work.

Reluctantly he let his own pet bird off his finger into its cage: a little white-cheeked Himalayan bulbul with a black crest, a saucy confident eye and a bright yellow vent under its tail. 'There. Go in, my jewel! Light of my eyes!' said Mahomed Iqbal. The floor of the cage was sanded; it was large and clean; there was fresh seed, fresh drinking water in the china cups; a spray of oleander was stuck in the netting at the side; there was a swing and a coconut shell. 'Little Prince. Darling,' said Mahomed Iqbal.

On the cobbles outside the shop, he had put down, for the fresher air, a wire cage in which there were three little she-monkeys, newly come on the Express from Assam. They clung together in the middle of the cage and had not unwound their arms from one another since they came off the train; one of them had her head hidden in the neck of the next. There was, too, a mongoose a boy had just brought in; Mahomed Iqbal had no time to attend to it now, he had to say his prayers, but a rag was bound tightly round its throat and Mahomed Iqbal was able to fasten it with a chain by pushing the clasp well into the little sinewy neck though the mongoose shrieked. The other end of the chain he slipped under the leg of a cage of birds, little bright munias brought in by the score from the forests. The birds, who had still not learned they were caged, flew up in fright and hit the wires. The mongoose met jerk after jerk of the chain as it ran its length in paroxysms of fear; it ran and fell and ran and fell on the concrete floor, its red eyes senseless. Minute black and copper-coloured feathers floated out of the birdcage on to the floor, torn off by the wires; a few of the birds lay stunned at the bottom of the cage, and all the while Mahomed Iqbal's bulbul called to him, 'Wheet-tre-trippy-wit-trippy-wit-trippy-wit!' Mahomed Iqbal's face broke into a broad smile.

'On the other hand,' wrote Ganesh, 'the Vedic writers, the old Mogul poets, sought to influence our stream of consciousness by pinpricks of suggestion, as the physician injects into the bloodstream his drug!' He read that over and as a sentence it pleased him. I am not writing only from my own point of view, thought Ganesh. Personally I consider the Mogul poets had no insight at all but I shall not say so, and feeling much ennobled he returned to his theme from which, he felt, he had wandered a little. 'But "drug", as a simile, is an anomaly to love,' he read aloud. 'Let us rather speak of love as the oil that makes the world's machinery turn smoothly; as the butter that binds the cake.'

'Butter?' asked Gurudas doubtfully and he said, 'I *wish* you would help me decide, Ganesh. What a smell that dustbin has. I think you should call Sushil to come away.'

Ganesh stood up lazily and stretched. His skin showed brown and smooth through the fine muslin of his shirt, the strands of the sacred thread he wore made a raised line across his chest, over his left shoulder, under his right armpit. The folds of his muslin *dhoti* swept gracefully round his ankles; he wore glossy patent-leather shoes that seemed to match his glossy well-oiled hair. 'Sushil, Sushil,' he called carelessly and sat down again. 'He does not hear,' he said.

'You don't care for your brother at all,' grumbled Gurudas.

The sun had gone down. Dusk had fallen in the square and lanes, the Indian dusk that is there for a moment and then gone. The cars had lights now and the myriad midget lanterns of the rickshaws were like fireflies while, in the shops, every tone of light shone, electric bulbs, acetylene flares and the soft flickering homely light of a cotton wick in a cup of oil.

The shops overflowed with goods, Indian and Occidental: shoes and fruit and jewels and Thermos flasks; lampshades and medicines; saucepans, taffeta cushions, handkerchiefs, catheters, photograph frames and toys; bath-towels, cottons and silks; frozen carcases, letter-writing paper, sweets, clocks, vegetables and luggage. The young wife of the Englishman could be seen threading the crowd in the centre aisle as her car had threaded the traffic outside. 'I have to get some embroidery silks, Hugh,' she had said. 'Give me some money.'

He gave her a ten-rupee note. 'I had better wait here with Nibs. He doesn't like a crowd,' and he waited outside, near the car rank, while she passed Sushil on her way to the entrance. Sushil looked up at her as he ran; in one glance he had noticed the oddness, to him, of her light hair, of the wet heat on her temples, her pink flushed cheeks, the flowered, rather harsh material of her short dress, her bare legs and large white shoes. She did not notice the little boy at all but Sushil's eyes had taken all of her in.

Now the people were eddying round the shops in a bright stream; they were buying and selling, talking and laughing and bargaining; pleading, arguing, shouting, whispering, disagreeing and agreeing. There were a thousand things among them that spoke of Ganesh's human love! Their looks at one another, their contacts shy or bold; it spoke in the books laid out on the bookstalls and from the enormous cinema hoardings. There were innumerable expressions of love in the jewels, toys, gifts and flowers on the stalls. There was religious love: Chérie, for instance, wore a gold cross on a chain. Love was in the preparation for the Hindu Puja and in the colour of Mahomed Iqbal's beard that, as it was dyed sorrel red, showed that he had made the Hāj, the holy pilgrimage to Mecca. 'To achieve individual love,' wrote Ganesh, 'the personality must be heightened; to achieve universal love, it must be lost.' 'But that is true,' said Ganesh in surprise and, much encouraged, he went on: 'Then slip as the thirsty river slips out into the mighty sea of selfless impersonal love.'

'*Can* you call a river thirsty?' asked irritating old Gurudas.

The Englishman, Hugh, waited good-temperedly on the edge of the crowd while his beautiful well-brushed little dog licked its parts at his feet. Those chance few words that Hugh had spoken to Sue of home, of England, had suddenly conjured up in him a wave of homesickness – heather, Cornish butter, fishing, ale – yet with it, never to leave him again, was the pull of this land of India that he served as he had never served his own.

The woman by the garbage heap had sat down on the cobbles with her baby and, holding it, was trying to turn its head to look at her, with her hand against its cheek. The baby looked at her, its face turned to her breast, then it lolled back, its eyes rolling up to look at the clouds again.

Under Hugh's arm was a folded newspaper; every day in its columns was printed the number of street destitutes admitted to hospital, the number of deaths. Hugh and his wife, Gurudas Dey and Ganesh, Mrs de Souza, even Mahomed Iqbal, knew what was in those columns. Now the woman sat trying to wake some spark in her baby as Mrs de Souza, Chérie and José at last reached the flower shops' range, and Mahomed Iqbal, smiling at his bulbul's chirrup, was ending his prayer. Sue was buying her silks and old Gurudas, having finally made up his mind for the earrings, had entered on the stage of bargaining with the shopkeeper. Sushil still ran from the shop to the car to the shop while Ganesh added a further sentence to his thesis of love. 'Once acquired, these erudite notions . . . '

'Fifty rupees!' groaned Gurudas. 'That is impossible. Ganesh, you should listen, I think, when I spend so much on your wife.'

'Bapu,' cried Sushil running in. 'Come. You must come. There is a woman, Bapu, crying because her baby is dead. Oh, Bapu!' Sushil was crying himself.

'Shocking,' said old Gurudas. 'Shocking.'

'Bapu, you must come. Its eyes are still open but it is dead. Poor woman. Come,' and he tugged at Gurudas.

'*Nahin. Nahin.* I cannot come. My legs pain me and I have all this to attend to. Besides what could I do if I came?' and, 'How can I think?' broke out Ganesh. 'How if you keep interrupting? Here, give her eight annas and tell her to go home.'

When Sushil came back, Gurudas stroked the boy's tear-stained ardent face. 'Leave her be now. This is festival time. No sad thoughts. Stay here, quietly with me. See, do you think Sitara will like these earrings?'

In the flower range Mrs de Souza and Chérie were choosing the wreath. José naturally did not choose; she had, cautiously, lowered the shopping bag so that it rested on the floor; her fingers were numb from its straps.

'Show me a handsome wreath,' said Mrs de Souza. 'It is for the funeral of Dr Domel.'

151

'We have sent many wreaths today for Dr Domel,' said the young shopkeeper.

'Dr Domel was a *great* friend of mine, m'n,' said Mrs de Souza, raising her voice so that it carried the length of the flower range. 'A veree great friend. He would have stood godfather to my little girl only he was prevented, but neither did he stand for Mrs Swindon's child, and he gave to my Chérie this cross and chain she wears,' Chérie bridled importantly. 'He was a veree great friend,' said Mrs de Souza. 'So show me a handsome wreath.'

'None that we supplied was as beautiful as this,' said the shopkeeper, and he displayed a massive wreath of gladioli lettered in silver 'God is Love' and tied with purple ribbon.

'Oh, Mummee!' said Chérie.

'It is a little crushed,' said Mrs de Souza carefully trying to disparage it. She walked round it and bumped into José. 'Dear God, José, why do you stand there stuck like a pole, m'n? I shall slap you, I promise. And pick up the bag. Do you need to put it there on the dirty floor, m'n?'

'Couldn't we get a coolie boy?' asked José in a faint voice.

'What? Spend two annas on a coolie when we have the use of our arms and legs? How much did you say the wreath was?' Mrs de Souza turned to the shopkeeper. 'Twelve rupees?'

'*Twelve?* Thirty!'

'*Thirtee!* Take it away.'

'At the very least, twenty-nine.'

'Twenty-nine! Dear God. Did you hear that? José, if you do not stand up, really I must slap you. Thirteen.'

'Twenty-eight.'

It was of no use. The real price of the wreath, it appeared, was twenty rupees and Mrs de Souza could not afford to pay more than sixteen. The gap was too large. The shopkeeper had to put it away and bring out another wreath of tuber-roses and white ribbon.

'But it is nutting as nice as the other,' whined Chérie.

The sum, 'twenty rupees', had arrested José's attention. They had talked, long ago, of her staying at school. 'Another year', her teacher had said, 'and she will pass her exams,' but the fees were twenty rupees a term and, 'I am not paying that,' Mrs de Souza had declared. José had to leave. Twenty rupees was too much to pay for weeks of teaching yet not too much for one wreath of flowers for someone who, if he were as good as José did not question Dr Domel had been, could gather flowers for himself in heaven. But I must not think such things; it is wicked, thought José and, straight away, as sometimes happens, a momentary quietness swept through the flower range; for a few seconds nobody spoke and, into the pause, came the sound of the church bell as it started again, ding-dong-dong. It was only ringing for evening Mass but to José it was a sign and she trembled. Mrs de Souza, unpinning the ten-rupee notes she had fastened to the lining of her bag with a safety pin, paused too and said, 'How lovelee to hear the bell, like a blessing for Dr Domel and for us who are buying the wreath,' and with the hand that now held the notes she crossed herself.

'But, Mummee!' came Chérie's shrill voice. 'Look. Look. There is Mrs Swindon's wreath!'

'Where?' Mrs de Souza turned sharply. 'Show me. Show me at once,' and her face fell. 'Dear God. How hideous!' she tried to say. 'How uglee!'

'How big!' said Chérie. 'How grand!'

Then Mrs de Souza lost her temper. 'Bring out the other wreath,' she cried. 'The first you showed me. Even if I am

to be robbed, shall I be shamed, m'n? *I* was the friend of
Dr Domel. Twenty rupees! Mrs Swindon would not have
paid half as much and here you take it from me! Twenty
rupees! And just now! *Now*, when everything is so dear.
Chérie, your dancing class is not paid for and you have no
winter vests; Father Joseph, himself, spoke to me about
your clothes, José, as if I could help that. How am I, I
ask you, to provide for a husband's sister's child, m'n?'
and, furious, she said to the shopkeeper, 'Take the money,
you robber, and at least put the card where everyone can
see. How shall we live? How can we? And then you, José,
ask me for coolies!' In an access of anger she gave José the
slap she had promised, right across the cheek.

'Our thoughts should lead us in the light of understanding,' wrote Ganesh, 'past the gold pillars (or obstacles) of
earthly love that can be classified, viz: man to woman (sex),
mother to child (maternal), brotherly (fraternal), father to
son (paternal, filial).'

'I want to go home,' said Gurudas. 'I want someone
to rub my legs.'

'Be quiet! Be quiet,' cried Ganesh, sharply. 'Now
I have forgotten what it was that I had to say.'

Hugh reminded Sue that they needed birdseed for
the budgerigar they had not long ago brought from
Mahomed Iqbal and they walked towards the separated
building where all the livestock was sold, everything alive
from little fluttering darts of birds to the droves of goats for
the butchers. From the building came a strong stench and a
noise that might superficially have been called chattering,
the multiple crying of terrified wild small hopeless voices.
Sue stopped.

'Hugh, I *can't* go in. I can't bear it.'

His eyes, kinder still, regarded her. 'No. Why should

you?' he said at once. 'Stay here. I'll go. You keep Nibs. He doesn't like it either.'

He gave her the leash and went into the shop.

'My bulbul, Sahib, has learned to ring his bell,' said Mahomed Iqbal proudly.

The Englishman's face lit up; here was something he could admire.

'See, when his seed is finished he taps the bell with his beak and it rings. I taught him,' said Mahomed Iqbal.

'And he is well?'

'Quite well. Very well. Little rascal!'

Mahomed Iqbal saw Hugh looking at the little she-monkeys. 'They are pretty,' he said. 'I thought I might get a price for them as pets,' and he added in English, 'Many sahibs buying little pets, but see, they are not friendly.'

He took a stick and rattled it on the cage. The monkeys did not move; the one with its face hidden, huddled closer, its forearm tightened round the others' necks; one raised its eyes to look up at Hugh but the eyes were vacant with fright, bright, beautifully shaped as almond shells. The third gave a cry and the sound brought, all along the range of pet shops, a fluttering up of birds and, from the heaped monkey cages, dark skinny hands holding the bars, little furred pinched faces looking out. Hugh, with his packet of seed, went hurriedly away.

'General love,' wrote Ganesh. After some hesitation he added '(kindly impersonal, usual).' He considered 'usual', almost crossed it out. 'But it *is* usual,' said Ganesh. All the same he tried again: 'Kindly impersonal love, interpolated . . . ' He considered that thoughtfully, then doubtfully, and looked up 'interpolated' in the pocket dictionary he carried, scratched the word out and wrote 'interpolitic' instead. That was quite true. True, he thought uneasily. It was all true but somehow it still was not truth.

'Bapu, that woman is still there. She is still crying.'

'Shocking,' said Gurudas again. 'They shouldn't allow such things to happen, especially in Puja time. It is most distressing. Ganesh, I must go home. My legs ache very much.'

'One moment. One moment,' said Ganesh. 'I have to write the sum up.'

Mahomed Iqbal called his assistant to bring his handcart; on it was a large cage and, with other animal-shop owners, they began the task of transferring chosen monkeys from the shop cages to the large one for the weekly dispatch. A sound of terror arose. The tiny hands clung to the very bars they had hated; males and females clung to one another and were dragged apart. Small monkeys became separated from their mothers. There were rending screams and struggles until the cage was filled and two coolies stood ready to trundle it away. As an afterthought Mahomed Iqbal picked up the cage of the three she-monkeys and emptied them, still sealed together, into the big cage and slammed and locked the door. 'To the Medical College,' said Mahomed Iqbal.

A heavy sacred bull was making its way slowly through the traffic of the square towards the garbage heap. It calmly shouldered the woman, who had risen with her baby, out of its way; the woman submitted and was pushed aside; the fat contented bull went past her as, happy again, Sushil ran finally out to the car with the earrings in their red velvet case.

Mrs de Souza's wreath lay ready for dispatch with its prominent card; the sound of José's sobbing had long ago left the flower range. Hugh and Sue had driven away with the little dog Nibs between them.

The handcart with the cage of monkeys was trundling towards the Medical College. The mongoose, exhausted, was limp now and Mahomed Iqbal was able to shut it in a wooden box with holes in the lid; he gave it a saucer of milk and an apple – pets must be kept in good condition. What he did not know was that presently, during the night, it would gnaw its way out and escape – a mongoose is seldom a victim – but the assistant had gathered up the bodies of the fallen munias and thrown them outside where they would swiftly be scavenged by the pariah dogs; meanwhile Mahomed Iqbal had carefully covered his bulbul's cage for the night.

The woman was trying to find somewhere to put her baby. She had eight annas now and could eat; the annas were safely tied where all poor Indian women keep their money, in a knot at the end of her sari, tucked in at her waist. She was pushed and shouldered aside as she had been by the bull but, at last, in the flower range she found an empty outside window-sill and laid the baby's body there; some leaves had fallen on the ground from the auspicious mango-leaf garlands strung for the festival; she gathered them up and covered the baby with the green; then, with a sob like a hiccup she turned away. In the lane beside the market were the cheap cook-shops but the smell of the food made her faint. 'Tell her to go home,' Ganesh had said; she had no home but the pavement and there she fell. At once, one of the avid shadows that had hovered by the garbage heap came swiftly and, with quick fingers, undid the knot at her waist – they knew exactly where to find it – and took the eight annas.

'Come along. Come along. Be quick. Sum it up,' said Gurudas to Ganesh. 'Come. Sushil is in the car. We must go home.'

Ganesh was reading over the pages he had written, pages of close writing, hundreds of words, all relevant, all true, all carefully thought out.

'Mercy, pity, peace and love: the nature of human love,' he read and was suddenly filled with despair.

'Go on. Hurry. Sum it. Sum it,' cried old Gurudas.

'But . . . I *cannot* sum it up,' said Ganesh.

Afterword

These last two stories, 'Miss Passano' and 'Mercy, Pity, Peace and Love', are alike because Jon and I felt intensely about many of the same things. What lies behind them is, I think, compassion – or lack of compassion – a 'sharing' even in cruelty, horror and grief because, if an author is trying to achieve what we early learned to call 'truthful writing', this 'sharing', whether we shrink from it or not, is the source of all creative inspiration, however small.

The stories are written in the past tense but, as I have said, both could be happening in exactly the same way today: Miss Passano's racking rickshaw journey over Howrah Bridge and the hot streets of Calcutta; Ganesh trying to write an over-ambitious thesis, his father buying presents he cannot afford in the Newmarket for the Puja festival; the ebb and flow of life though, sadly, every year there are more beggars round the garbage heaps, more dying babies, more suffering animals. It was the same when I was a child and will be the same when I am long gone but, then, the Hindi word for yesterday and tomorrow is the same.

R. G.

Acknowledgments

STORIES

'Possession': Mooltiki;* Commonwealth Anthology for Schools, 1958; Times of India

'The Oyster': The New Yorker, 1950; Winter's Tales, Macmillan; Mooltiki.

'Sister Malone and the Obstinate Man': Colliers magazine; Harpers magazine.

'The Wild Duck': Mooltiki.

'Red Doe': Colliers magazine; Mooltiki; read by Danish Broadcasting Corporation, 1958; The Saturday Book, Collins.

'The Little Black Ram': Mooltiki; Commonwealth Anthology for Schools, 1958; Times of India

Mercy, Pity, Peace and Love': Tomorrow's magazine in abridged form.

'Miss Passano': Story magazine.

POEMS

Bengal River: Mooltiki; Guinness Book of Poetry, 1956–7.

Kashmir Winter: Mooltiki.

* Mooltiki, Macmillan, 1957; Viking, 1958; reprinted 1966.